THE SNOTTLE

Michael Lawrence

Illustrated by Ellis Nadler

First published in 2003
by Orchard Books
This Large Print edition published by
BBC Audiobooks Ltd
by arrangement with
Watts Publishing Group Ltd
2005

ISBN 1 4056 6051 1

Text copyright © Michael Lawrence 2003
Illustrations © Ellis Nadler 2003

British Library Cataloguing in Publication Data

Lawrence, Michael
  The Snottle.—Large print ed.
  1. McCue, Jiggy (Fictitious character)—Juvenile
fiction 2. Humorous stories 3. Children's stories
  4. Large type books
  I. Title II. Nadler, Ellis
  823.9'14[J]

ISBN 1-4056-6051-1

Printed and bound in Great Britain by
Antony Rowe Ltd., Chippenham, Wiltshire

For John Rowland Prest
critic, commentator and friend
for an alarming number of years

CHAPTER ONE

My mother has this really disgusting habit. Every time she blows her nose she opens out the hanky and looks at the result. 'Why do you do that?' I yell. 'What do you expect to see in there? A missing earring? A cream cake? A doorway into *Narnia*?'

'I have bad sinuses,' she says.

'I have a bad haircut,' I say, 'but do you catch me looking at it in a hanky? Don't *do* it, please.'

But she carries on doing it, every time. Gets right up my nose.

Why am I telling you this? Because of something that happened to me and Pete and Angie which had quite a lot to do with the stuff that slurps out of hooters. It started with this new girl in class. Her name was Steffany, Steff for short, but everyone—well, the boys—called her Snonker. We called her Snonker because every now and then she would make this great honking noise and this horrible gloop would

1

leap out of her nose in twin streams. You could never tell when a snonk was coming. There was no warning. There you'd be, eyes closed, pretending you were anywhere but in class, when this hair-raising hoot would rip you out of your seat and turn your heart into a tom-tom. Steff kept a hanky the size of a tablecloth up her sleeve like a spare muscle and usually managed to catch the stuff, but sometimes she missed and it hit her desk, or the floor, or the neck of the person in front. Then she would mop it up, all frantic, like she didn't want anyone to see it. If she'd been my mother she would have been examining her work for an hour.

But it wasn't just the snonking that got us about Steff. Even when she wasn't snonking, she was sniffing. Her nose never seemed to stop running. When the class was quiet, apart from the snores, all you could hear was this sniff-sniff-sniff in the background, and when you looked around you saw that everybody was sitting at their desks with clenched fists. Bryan Ryan stood up once and screamed at her through

2

his rolled-up maths book, and for once he wasn't given detention or sent out. You could tell by the look in their eyes that the teachers wished they could shout at her too, but they didn't dare in case she sued them.

'Bad cold you have there, Steffany,' Miss Weeks said in one lesson. 'Have you taken anything for it?'

'Like rat poison?' said Pete, who sits next to me.

'I've tried everything,' Snonker sniffled. 'The doctor says it's some sort of allergy, or something in the air round here that doesn't agree with me.'

'You can get pills and sprays for most allergies,' Miss Weeks said.

'I've tried stacks, Miss. Nothing works.'

'Well, let's hope you find something that *does* work—soon.'

None of the boys had spoken to Snonker since she arrived, but a couple of the girls had, including Angie Mint. Angie's our best mate. Pete's and mine. We overlook the fact that she's a girl because we've known her all our lives and have kind of got used to it. But we

3

draw the line, a very thick line, at rubbing shoulders with other girls, so when Angie said we ought to be nicer to Snonker—this was one afternoon on the way home from school—she didn't get a whoop of joy from either of us.

'Nicer to her?' Pete said. 'I couldn't *be* nicer to her.'

'You don't even talk to her,' said Angie.

'And that's as nice as I'm getting. That girl is an alien.'

'Alien?'

'From another school, another town.'

'She'll never be one of us if we don't let her in,' Angie said.

'Let her in?' I said.

'I've been thinking it's about time we expanded the Musketeers.'

We stared at her. '*Bring someone else into the Musketeers*?!'

'Yes. Why not?'

'Well, for starters,' I said, 'we're the *Three* Musketeers.'

'One for all and all for lunch,' said Pete.

'Exactly. You can't have *four* people

in the Three Musketeers. Want to borrow my calculator?'

'I feel sorry for her,' Angie said. 'She only has her mum, she's just moved here, and she has no friends.'

'Well she's not having this one,' said Pete.

'Look,' I said suddenly. 'Joggers.'

'Huh?' said Angie.

'Joggers. There.'

Three men in tracksuits were running in step along the horizon.

'What about them?' Angie asked.

'I don't get joggers,' I said. 'They go out all hours, all weathers. They get out of breath, sweat like pigs, look like they're about to keel over any minute, and they wear stupid clothes to do it all in. Can that be *normal*?'

We watched the three joggers running lower and lower into the ground until Pete said:

'Why did they move here anyway?'

'Who?' Angie said.

'Snonker and her old lady.'

'Oh, something about her nan dying and leaving her cottage to Steff's mum and Steff's mum not wanting it and

5

buying another place nearby instead,' Angie said.

'Glad I asked,' said Pete.

She scowled at him. 'How would you like it if you moved to a new town and another school and didn't know a soul and no one spoke to you?'

He beamed. 'Bliss.'

'What are we doing here?' I said.

'You mean, what is humanity's purpose on Earth, in the universe, in the great scheme of things?' Angie said.

'No, I mean how did the three of us get to this rubbish dump?'

We'd strayed from our usual boring route home to another boring one. On our right there was this enormous mountain of rubbish, known locally as the Midden, a kind of unofficial dump, which is uglier than sin and stinks like . . . well, a rubbish dump. The official council tip is just round the corner, up a dirt track, but a lot of people can't be bothered to go the extra hundred metres and sort their rubbish into the enormous skips provided (each with its own luminous label telling you what

6

you can put in it), so the Midden gets bigger and bigger and stinkier and stinkier all the time.

'What's that?' said Pete.

'What's what?' I said.

'That.'

There was something unusual in the Midden. Something small and round that was watching us go by. We stopped.

'Looks like a grapefruit,' Angie said. 'A green grapefruit.'

'Grapefruits don't have eyes,' I said.

'I said *like* a grapefruit.'

'Not very,' I said.

'The Creature of the Midden,' said Pete.

'What?' said Ange.

'Haven't you heard The Legend of the Creature of the Midden?'

'No.'

Neither had I. 'Where did you hear it?' I asked.

'Hear what?' said Pete.

'The Legend of the Creature of the Midden.'

'I never heard it.'

'You just said you had.'

'No, I didn't. I said, "Haven't you heard The Legend of the Creature of the Midden?" not that there was one.'

'So there isn't any such legend?'

'Not that I know of.'

As I gripped my skull to stop it flying off into space, I heard a voice. Angie's. She was moving slowly towards the thing that didn't look much like a grapefruit with her hand outstretched.

'Here, Creature,' she said. 'Come to Angie.'

'Oh yeah, like it speaks English,' Pete said.

Angie started making these coochie-coo noises, but the creature just looked suspicious.

'If it snuggles up to you,' Pete said, 'don't expect to come near me.'

'She probably wasn't planning to,' I said.

'Quiet,' Angie said. 'You'll scare it off.'

'Good idea,' said Pete, and started jumping up and down, shouting 'Ooh-waw, eeeee, wo-wo-wo, hoppit-hoppit-hoppit!'

The creature that wasn't the

Creature of the Midden pulled back. Muck and rubbish fell like a garage door over the place where it had been.

Angie ran back to Pete, turned his shoulder to mashed potato with a single fist, and flounced homeward without us.

CHAPTER TWO

It was almost seven o'clock and the McCue family were sprawling in front of the TV. There wasn't much point to this as the TV had decided not to work any more just before tea, but old habits die hard.

'That's what you get for buying cheap,' Mum said, giving Dad one of her It's-your-fault looks.

'You wanted to buy a TV, not me,' Dad said. 'I was happy to go on renting. We've rented for years without any problems.'

'I get sick of throwing money away on rentals,' Mum said.

'I get sick of throwing money away on getting things repaired,' said Dad.

With the telly kaput, you'd think we'd be stuck for something to do, but not so. Mum was leafing slowly through the latest Argos Catalogue like she was trying to memorise it, Dad was having his fifth go at a book Oliver Garrett had lent him called something

10

like *How To Make Oodles of Loot Without Actually Getting Off Your Big Fat Bum*, and I was working on my Art Project, a strip cartoon called *Captain Neasden, Superprat*.

'Whatever next?' Mum said suddenly from the Argos Catalogue. 'Cufflinks for wedding personnel. They have their titles engraved in them.'

'Oh yes?' said Dad, as interested as a sock.

'Yes. Best Man, Usher, Groom.'

'What's an Usher?' I asked.

'Person who brings the ice cream,' Dad said.

When she got to the end of the catalogue, Mum dropped it on the floor and reached for last week's free local rag. Silence for a full twenty seconds while she trawled the fascinating front page for gossip, then:

'The west wing of the church has been burnt down—deliberately!'

'Wasn't me,' Dad said, turning his book upside down to see if it made more sense that way.

'By vandals!' said Mum.

'Well, I didn't think it was new

11

converts.'

'This isn't funny, Mel. They should be banned.'

'Churches? Couldn't agree more.'

'Vandals.'

He looked over his book. 'As opposed to actively encouraged, you mean?'

'It's all one big joke to you, isn't it,' she snapped. 'You don't care that society's crumbling about our ears. God, I hate vandals!'

'Hate is a very strong word,' I said in the deep, manly voice of Captain Neasden, Superprat.

'What?'

'That's what you tell me whenever I say I hate something. "Jiggy," you say, "Hate is a very strong word," you say.'

'Well, so it is. And I hate vandals. They ought to be locked up.'

'You can't lock up every vandal,' Dad said. 'The prisons are already bursting at the seams with more deserving cases.'

'So what's your solution? Free DVDs of their favourite films to keep them off the streets?'

12

'If that was on offer I'd be out there with a spray can and a box of matches myself.'

'You're a bad influence on that boy,' my mother said.

'What boy?'

'Him. Your son.'

'Don't bring me into this,' I said.

'Children take a lot of notice of what their parents do,' Mum said sternly.

'Do you take a lot of notice of what I do?' Dad said to me.

'No,' I said.

'No worries there then.'

'And litter louts,' Mum said.

'Litter louts?' Dad and I said together.

'They should be fined. Heavily. And if they do it again, they should be put away with the vandals, in special prisons with vandalised cells and litter all over the place. Then they'd know what it's like.'

I made a mental note never to vandalise anything or drop stuff while my mother was about. If I did, the postman would probably find my head on a spike beside the gate next

13

morning.

I shoved Captain Neasden back in his folder, put my invisible super-cape on, said, 'Up, up, and away!' and flew across the road to Pete and Angie's with one eye on the traffic. Did I mention that P & A live in the same house even though they're not related? It's their parents, her mum, his dad. They have this thing going: she cleans his car, he burns most of the food. Seems to work.

Audrey let me in. Audrey is Angie's mum. I went straight up as ordered— after a bit of cheek. I'll have to tell her off for that one of these days. Pete and Angie were in their rooms watching TV. Separate rooms, separate TVs, which really rubbed it in. If I'd had a TV in my room I could be watching too, instead of being driven out by loopy Golden Oldie chat. But am I allowed a TV in my room? No I'm not. One of the many rules of the tyrant I call Mother.

I went to Angie's first because it's nearest from the top of the stairs and the door was half open. 'What's

cooking?' I said.

'Nothing,' she said.

'Want to go for a walk?'

'Not particularly.'

I ambled along the landing to Pete's room, kicked the door back, and stood there with rippling muscles, fists like pineapples. He wasn't impressed. As well as the TV, he had a CD on and was blowing things up on his computer.

'Whatcha doing?' I asked.

'Destroying the enemy.'

'What enemy?'

'Any enemy.'

'Want to go for a walk?'

'Nah.'

I unrippled the mighty muscles, de-pineappled the mighty fists, and flipped through the TV channels. There was nothing on.

'Come on,' I said. 'Let's get outta here.'

He blew up a few more enemies and sat back in his swivel.

'Well, I've wiped most of 'em out anyway.'

We collected Ange on the way. She was bored, too, so she didn't need

much persuading. Out on the front step, Pete told us to wait a mo and went round the back. A minute later he returned wheeling his new bike.

'We're going for a walk, not a ride,' I said.

'Walking's for wimps!' he said, slinging a leg over the saddle and shooting along the pavement, kicking the NO RIDING BIKES ON THE PAVEMENT sign as he went. We followed him through the estate. When we came to the big yellow-and-rust council skip with FOR RESIDENTS ONLY on the side, I stood on my toes and looked in. No residents.

Pete was waiting for us at the main road, still in the saddle, leaning against a lamppost, arms folded over his weedy chest. 'Where to?'

We shrugged. 'Don't mind.'

Trouble was, we'd been everywhere. We thought of going into town, but decided that there's only so much of a thrill you can get from looking in closed shop windows and playing hopscotch round the doggy doodahs, and sloped off in another direction

16

entirely. Pete took the lead, naturally, sometimes with his hands stretched out like a trapeze artist, sometimes with them behind his head like a berk. 'If two's company and three's a crowd,' he yelled back at us, 'what are four and five?'

'Nine!' I yelled back.

'You've heard it!'

'We had the same lousy Christmas crackers!'

'All right, name three keys that don't unlock doors!'

'Monkey, turkey, donkey!' I yelled.

'Wrong! Turkey, donkey, monkey! What goes ho-ho-ho-thud?'

I wasn't sure about this one. '. . . Father Christmas punching a reindeer?'

'No! Someone laughing his stupid head off!'

'What goes on and on and never stops?' yelled Angie.

'Pete Garrett!' I yelled.

Pete whizzed on ahead and I started to wish I'd come on my bike too. The main reason I hadn't is that I don't have one. My mother says that if I

17

don't have a bike, I can't get knocked off it. I have a deprived childhood. No TV in my bedroom, no bike, a mother whose middle name is Führer.

'Ever wish you had a bike, Ange?' I asked as we cruised along on foot some way behind Pete.

'No,' she said.

'Why's that then?'

'Can't really talk while you're riding a bike.'

'No, s'pose not,' I said.

After that we ran out of things to say.

CHAPTER THREE

Civilisation ended in a while and we came to the slope down to Ingle Woods. Pete got down it first, feet on pedals, back-end trying for a tan. 'Looka this,' he said, as we zimmered after him. He meant the big sign that wasn't there last time we came this way.

SITE ACQUIRED FOR CONSTRUCTION OF FIFTY FOUR BEDROOM ARCHITECT DESIGNED EXECUTIVE HOMES

'Fifty-four bedrooms?' Pete said, riding round us, hands on hips.

'Fifty,' I said slowly, so he stood a chance of getting it, 'four-bedroom,' I added, even more slowly, 'architect-designed,' I went on, a syllable every three seconds, 'executive homes,' I

19

finished like a weary snail.

'Homes!' Angie said. 'Why do they always say that?'

'You want them to lie?' I asked. 'You want them to say they're building executive rabbit hutches? Executive birdcages? Executive prison cells?'

'I want them not to say "home". A house isn't a home until there's furniture and people in it.'

'What is an executive home anyway?' Pete asked.

'A home for executives,' I explained.

'House,' said Ange.

'It's the "architect designed" that gets me,' Pete said. 'I mean who else would design them? Milkmen? PE teachers? Pizza delivery boys?'

He stopped circling and slapped his feet on the ground. Spread his hands to show us the invisible sign in his head.

'Roadsweeper-designed executive homes.'

'Houses,' said Angie.

'Bus-driver-designed executive homes,' Pete said.

'HOUSES!' said Angie, kicking his front wheel.

20

'Librarian-designed executive houses,' said Pete, pedalling away. 'Dinner-lady-designed executive houses. Car-park attendant-designed executive h—'

'All right, Pete, all right, we get it,' I said.

But he didn't stop. He went on and on with somebody-designed executive houses as he sped over the bumpy ground. Ange and I strolled after him, kicking squashed lager cans along the rim of the woods, till we came to a bunch of trees with these bright orange posters all over them. Same poster, different trees.

RESPECT THIS TREE
TREES HAVE FEELINGS TOO
The Fellowship of Ancient Rights
for Trees
is watching YOU!

The Fellowship of Ancient Rights for Trees, FART for short, was everywhere these days. FARTers didn't like the idea of things being done to trees. Their greatest enemies were tree fellers (fellas who lop trees), and they picketed wood yards up and down the country, and spray-painted the windows of DIY stores that sell wooden kitchens, and garden centres that sell bird tables and benches. Ordinary people with woody connections didn't escape either. There'd been a story on the news a few days ago about a tramp who had his wooden leg stolen while he slept in the doorway of an Oxfam shop. Some kids found it in the graveyard, buried in a leg-sized plastic coffin. It was the tombstone that gave it away. About A4 size, bearing the words, 'Rest in peace, friend.'

A little way beyond the last orange FART poster, Pete stopped to wait for us. 'Look,' he said, pointing a toe at a wad of people beside the road, where the wood ended. The wad looked like they'd just arrived and were sorting

themselves into some sort of order. When they were ready, they started to chant.

'HANDS OFF OUR ANCIENT TREES! HANDS OFF OUR ANCIENT TREES! HANDS OFF OUR ANCIENT TREES!'

'Protesters,' Angie said in case we'd mistaken them for window cleaners or ballet dancers.

Pete dismounted and we stepped into the wood so we could move closer, tree by tree, without being seen from the road. The chanting FARTers were now waving placards at passing motorists too busy talking illegally into their mobiles to notice them.

'Haven't they got anything better to do?' Pete said.

'The motorists?' I said.

'The FARTers.'

'They're concerned about the trees,' Angie said.

'They're only trees,' he said.

'You like trees,' I said.

'I do?' he said.

'Climbing them. Peeing against them when you think no one's looking.'

23

'I don't need a whole forest of the things.'

'So you'd rather see houses here, would you?' Angie said.

'People can live in houses,' Pete said.

'They can live in trees if they want,' I said.

'And plug the fridge and computer into . . . ?'

'There's a lot to be said for the simple life,' said Angie.

'As simple as no flush toilets?' Pete said.

'Well . . .'

'HANDS OFF OUR ANCIENT TREES! HANDS OFF OUR ANCIENT TREES! HANDS OFF OUR ANCIENT TR—!'

'Layabouts!' Pete yelled suddenly. 'Go home! Shove off!'

The FARTers broke off and turned to us with shocked expressions. That is they turned to Angie and me. Pete had ducked behind a tree.

One of the protesters raised his voice. 'Do you really want to see our historic woodlands destroyed to make way for more houses?'

24

Angie and I opened our mouths to say something friendly like, 'No, not really,' but before we could get it out Pete shouted from behind the tree— 'We don't give a squirrel's nut! Hope they bulldoze the lot!'—so that it looked as if it was us who'd spoken.

'I'll swing for him,' Angie said, through her teeth.

'Get in line,' I said, through mine.

Realising that they weren't going to get a change of heart out of us so long as Pete was putting words in our mouths, the protesters went back to their chanting. They'd just started when there was this almighty honk in their midst. The chanting died. Some of them moved aside, and we saw Steffany from class mopping her face with her enormous hanky.

'What's she doing with them?' Angie said.

I didn't care what the Snonker was doing with them. I was more interested in feeding Pete, limb by limb, to endangered species. 'Loonies,' he said as I went after him with outstretched hands. 'Ought to be put in a boat and

25

marooned on a desert island.'

'It's still a free country,' said another voice.

Pete stopped running and I stopped reaching for him. A middle-aged geezer in a tweed jacket, brown trousers and green suede shoes had stepped out from the trees.

'And they're not doing any harm,' he added.

'You never know what those nutters might do,' Pete said.

'Oh, they're just a bit worked up about the wood,' said the tweedy geezer.

'Are you one of them?' I asked him.

He laughed. 'No. But I defend their right to air their grievances.'

'Nothing better to do,' Pete said.

'Me?' said the tweedy type.

'Them.'

The geezer laughed again, and toddled off through the woods like he lived there.

'She's seen us,' Angie said.

'Who?' I said.

'Steff.'

And she had. She was waving at us

26

from the wad of protesters. Angie waved back. I didn't. Nor did Pete. We were making ourselves scarce before someone could shove a placard in our mitts and make us memorise the immortal words 'HANDS OFF OUR ANCIENT TREES!' in triplicate.

CHAPTER FOUR

We have lessons in a lot of different classrooms at Ranting Lane School, but if the teachers think the variety is going to bring a happy smile to our innocent faces they have another think coming. I mean, just as you get your feet up on one desk the bell goes, and you're expected to flip out into the corridor and charge off in this direction or that, hoping you don't get lost along the way. Or hoping you do. All the classrooms look pretty much the same anyway, so the novelty is somewhere round the ankles of zero.

The day after we went to Ingle Woods and met the tweedy type and listened to all the jolly FARTers, we had English with Mrs Gamble. It was afternoon. Everyone was in their usual seat except Marlene Bronson and Angie Mint. Angie usually sits next to Karen Mertz in English, but not today. Today Marlene was sitting next to Karen and Angie was sitting where

28

Marlene sat last week, shoulder to shoulder with Steff the Snonker. Angie explained afterwards. When Steff joined the class a week ago she was put in the empty seat next to Marlene, and Marlene didn't say a word to her all lesson but kept pinching her arm (finger-pinching, not stealing), and Ange felt kind of sorry for Snonker, and bribed Marlene to move. The bribe was half a box of left-over chocolate-covered hazelnuts. She knows Marlene can't resist chocolate-covered hazelnuts, even old ones. These were so old they'd forgotten what sort of nuts they were supposed to be, and the chocolate was grey, but Marlene didn't care.

Well there we were, all quiet and goody-goody (because Mrs Gamble is the Boss!) when suddenly there was a horrendous honk. Every cheek left its seat and Mrs G jumped backwards in surprise. Her chalk left her hand and said hello to the ceiling before coming down like a speeding peanut on the back of Pete's head. 'I didn't do anything!' he said, shoving his Game

29

Boy in his pocket.

But no one was interested in Pete. All eyes were on Steff, who'd almost snonked the windows out. Her desk was covered with slimy nose juice, and a pair of thick green strings hung from her nostrils: the kind of thing Tarzan uses to swing through the jungle and rescue Jane or some chimp.

'Hold still!' said Angie, trying to catch the swaying strings in a tissue. She gripped Snonker's nose and was still holding on when something on the desk caught her eye and she forgot everything. Steff reminded her. 'You're squeeding by doze,' she said.

Angie relaxed her grip and looked from the desk to where Mrs Gamble was smoothing her hair down behind the door. When she looked back at the desk she seemed puzzled. Steff started frantically mopping the desk with the enormous hanky from her sleeve. She was still mopping when the door flew back and pinned Mrs Gamble to the wall as Mother Hubbard, our Headteacher, ran in to see what the humungous noise had been. He would

30

have heard Steff's snonk already, but it was his first day back after a 'How-to-Be-a-Really-Cool-Head' course operated by the Ministry of Edu-something.

'What's going on here?' Mother bawled. 'Where's Mrs Gamble?'

'She's behiiiiiiind you!' several comedians chanted at once, but he didn't get it and before anyone could explain the bell went, which meant time to go, pronto. When he saw us coming, Hubbard gave a little whimper and sank into a crouch, arms over his head while we swarmed around him like a hive of bees on their way to Honey Break. *(Mrs G was still behind the door, probably feeling pretty flat about all this.)*

Out in the playground, Pete and I asked Ange what happened back there.

'I saw the future,' she said.

'The future?' I said. 'Um . . . how do you mean?'

'The stuff Steff's nose fired at the desk. There were pictures in it, moving pictures, showing Mrs Gamble standing by the door and the door

31

crashing back, and Hubbard coming in. The whole scene.'

'Are you telling us,' Pete said, 'that you saw what was going to happen and you saw it in . . . *snot*?'

'Yes.'

He opened his sleeve and laughed down it, like he does.

Angie turned to me. She looked like she needed a friend. Someone she could rely on. Someone who wouldn't laugh at her.

'You believe me, don't you, Jig?'

But I couldn't look at her. 'Well I . . .'

Her eyes shrank to black specks. 'You doubt me, after all the stuff that's happened to you, which I believed *totally* when you told me?'

'Not always totally, Ange.'

'I give you the benefit of the doubt more often than you deserve.'

'Yeah, but this takes some benefiting, you have to agree.'

'You want proof, is that it?'

'Proof would be cool.'

'Then watch what happens next time Steff snonks.'

32

'Rather not,' I said.

'You'll watch if I have to tear your eyes out and shove them in it one by one.'

'What a nerve,' said Pete, aiming his chin at the secluded corner of the playground we know as the Concrete Garden. We have a private bench in the Concrete Garden where we swap lunchtime crisps and sandwiches and improve the world. It wasn't lunchtime now, but that wasn't the point. Someone was sitting on our bench. Steff the Snonker.

'I think she's crying,' Angie said.

Pete snorted. 'Girls! Cry-babies!'

Angie grabbed his wrist and jerked it up behind his back.

'What was that?'

'Some girls,' Pete said.

She jerked harder. 'Sorry? My lugs are a bit duff today.'

'GIRLS ARE THE RULERS OF THE UNIVERSE!' he shrieked.

She let his arm drop. 'And don't you forget it.'

We headed for the Concrete Garden. Pete picked his arm up and

33

followed us, shaking it to get some feeling back into it. Snonker looked up as we approached the bench.

'Go 'way,' she said.

We didn't go away, but Pete and I kept our distance while Angie sat down next to her. This started Steff off again, sobbing like a maniac, but when she'd got it all out of her system Angie persuaded her that Pete and I weren't as bad as we looked and we joined them. We didn't sit, of course. It's OK to sit next to Angie, because she's a Musketeer, not an actual girl, but if we sat next to Steff and Bryan Ryan or some of the others saw us they would be taking the widdle out of us this time next year.

Because Angie was one of the few who'd bothered to make friends with her, Steff started to tell us about her sneezing and snotting.

'I sort of inherited it from my nan,' she said.

'Your nan used to snonk?' Pete said.

'Snonk?'

'Hoot loudly through the snout,' I explained.

34

'Snonk,' she said, turning the word over in her mind. 'Good word. Only Nan did it professionally.'

Pete smirked. 'Your nan was a professional snonker?'

'She told people's fortunes at fairs and things.'

'Are you saying . . .' (This was me) '. . . that she told people's fortunes with her *snot*?'

'Yes. It was a kind of gimmick, I suppose.'

'Some gimmick.'

She seemed happy to tell us everything now that she'd got going, but just then the bell rang for the last lesson of the day.

'Meet me after school,' Steff said, 'and I'll fill you in on the rest. But please. Keep it to yourselves. I don't want this getting round. People think I'm weird enough as it is.'

We swore, as good Musketeers, never to breathe a word to our dying day. I wonder if it counts, writing it down like this?

35

CHAPTER FIVE

Pete wasn't too keen on being seen with Steff out of school, so when we met her at the end of the afternoon, he jerked his jacket up over his head so no one would see his face. To make doubly sure they wouldn't see through his clever disguise, he slung the strap of his school bag round his neck, with the bag on his back like a hump. I didn't remind him about the two giant words on the bag. These words were made of silver studs that caught the sun and made total strangers read them over and over until their eyes rusted. The words were: PETE GARRETT.

On the way to nowhere in particular, Steff told us about her fortune-telling nan, starting with her stage name. Well, tent name.

'Come again?' said Angie.

'Nostrilamus. She called herself Nostrilamus.'

'As in Nostradamus?'

'Right,' said Steff, wiping her nose,

which was dripping.

'Nostra-whatus?' Pete asked from under his coat.

'Nostradamus,' I said. 'Eighteenth-century Italian astrologer.'

'Sixteenth-century French clair-voyant,' Steff said.

'He read fortunes in snot?' Pete said.

'Probably not in snot,' Steff said. 'But my nan did. Well, not fortunes exactly. When she snonked, pictures of what was going to happen appeared. It was a gift she had, and now I've got it, and I don't want it.'

'When did you start to snonk?' Angie asked.

'Just after Nan died and we moved here from Natherstock. My nose has been running ever since, and every now and then I . . .'

'Snonk.'

'Yes.'

'All over things.'

'Yes. It can be embarrassing. I try to catch it, but it comes so fast.'

'And you reckon you can see the future in it?' I said.

'Anyone can. But there has to be

37

someone else there or it's just ordinary snot.'

'Tee-hee-hee,' said Pete down the sleeve hooked over his left ear.

'I saw what was going to happen in the classroom,' Angie said.

'So you say,' said Pete.

Angie lifted his coat and scowled under it. 'Yes. So I say. You got a problem with that?' He didn't answer and she let his coat drop.

'Did your nan snonk into a hanky and look at the result?' I asked Steff, thinking of my mother's disgusting habit.

'No. She had this special plate. The Future Plate, she called it. She used it when paying customers wanted to know what was going to happen to them. She was always getting complaints, though, because the futures were never good and always just around the corner.'

'What sort of futures were they?'

'Oh, nothing brilliant. Falling over a cable, losing a toupee in a sudden wind, that sort of thing. Small stuff.'

'Did your nan snonk and sniff when

she wasn't working?' Angie asked.

Steff said she didn't know, but she was pretty sure that she only sniffed and snonked when she was in her Nostrilamus gear. 'She was a professional,' she added.

'Hey, it's them again,' I said.

'Who?' said Pete from under his coat.

'The joggers.'

It was the same three as yesterday, moving in perfect rhythm along the horizon.

'Fascinating,' he said, kicking a stone.

'What happened to the Fortune Plate?' Angie asked Steff.

'Future Plate,' Steff said. 'Mum threw it away after Nan died. It was just an old tin plate.'

'And the fortune-telling clobber?'

'Help the Aged.'

'My dad's favourite shop,' I said as the joggers fell over the far side of the horizon.

'I still have this though.'

She hoisted this greeny-brown thing that hung round her neck on a leather

shoelace and looked kind of like a big conker. I mean a conker case before it opens. It even had tiny little spikes all over it, but they weren't sharp. I touched them to see. Kind of furry. And there was a funny little loop on top of the thing, like the eye of a large needle. This was where the shoelace went.

'It's some sort of seed pod, we think,' Steff said. 'Nan used to call it her lucky charm, but I don't think it's special or anything. Except to me. It's the only thing I have of hers now *Ingle Nook* is sold.'

'*Ingle Nook*?' I said, wiping my nose, which had started to run. Not jog. Really run.

'Her cottage in the woods. Ingle Woods, where you saw me and the Fellowship of Ancient Rights for Trees yesterday.'

'The FARTers,' said Pete from under his coat.

'We joined them when we found out we'd been tricked,' Steff said.

'Tricked?' said Ange.

'Nan left the cottage to Mum in her

40

will, but Mum didn't want to live in the woods like some hermit. Also, there's no central heating, the electricity's dodgy, and the gas comes in canisters. Mum sold it and bought the house we're in now with the proceeds. What we didn't know was that the person who bought *Ingle Nook* planned to flatten it, along with the wood, and build a new housing estate. When Mum heard, she felt she'd been conned and wanted to try and get it stopped.'

'Well, look where we are again,' Pete said, peering through a sleeve at our surroundings.

We looked. For the second day in a row we'd come to the Midden.

'Must be something about it,' I said.

'There is,' he said. 'It stinks and it's ugly.'

A batch of seagulls was circling the dump, diving down, grabbing stuff in their beaks, and flying up again to gulp it. We're not near the sea, but the gulls often come inland. Maybe it gets boring flying over water all the time.

'I hope they don't like living things,' Angie said.

41

'Of course they do,' I said. 'They're called fish.'

She pointed to the small round head watching us from the dump.

I saw Steff's eyes widen. 'What is it?' she said.

'It's history,' said Pete.

He would have lobbed a stone at the Creature of the Midden but Angie stepped in front of him.

'Throw that,' she said, 'and *you* are history.'

'Uh-oh,' said Steff.

'Uh-oh what?' I said, turning to her.

Her face was all screwed up like she was trying to hold her teeth in, and she was fumbling up her sleeve for something that wasn't there.

'Where is it, where is it?'

'If you mean your snotty hanky,' Pete said, 'it fell out a while back.'

'Well, why didn't you say?' Angie said.

'No one asked m—'

If anything came after 'm', it didn't get heard, because Steff had snonked all over the face of the last person to turn to her and say 'Uh-oh what?'

42

CHAPTER SIX

For roughly nine point six seconds after Steff nosed the entire contents of her head on to my face, there was silence. During this silence I stood there, not blinking, and the others stood there, staring at me like I'd done something staggeringly clever instead of fail to duck.

Pete was the first to elbow the silence aside and stomp it into the ground. He let his coat and bag fall and leant forward to examine my dripping features.

'Hey, Jig,' he said, 'I can see the future. No wait, it's the past. Wow. Guess what. Somebody snonked all over you!'

Then he folded over in hysterics and Steff started saying, 'Sorry, sorry, sorry,' and I tried saying, 'It's OK, don't worry about it, it's all right,' except that somehow the words wouldn't come.

I was about to wipe my chops on

Pete's shirt, which was hanging out as usual, when something else landed on my face. Something that seemed to want to cut off my air supply and my vision and my sanity all at once. Pete stopped laughing and Steff and Ange squawked. I would have squawked too, but my face, including my mouth, was being licked by liquid sandpaper.

I tugged the thing off and held it at arm's length. It was round and green and reaching for my head with two tiny little hands with twitching fingers. It didn't have any legs or feet, and it was quite chirpy now, where before, in the Midden, it had looked a bit tired, or weak.

'Oh, isn't it sweet?' said Steff.

'Sweet?' I said, wondering if this was Russian for the words I would have used, which were 'disgusting' and 'uck!'

The creature in my hands must have liked the sound of Steff's voice because when she said 'Isn't it sweet?' it stopped drooling over me and swivelled its eyes to her. When it saw that her nose was running it jumped out of my hands, hit the ground, and

44

bounced up to her face like it had a spring under it. Steff gave another squawk, but once the creature was dangling from her cheeks and lapping her top lip she started giggling. 'Tickles,' she said as Pete, Angie and I clenched our faces as if someone had said: 'Eat that *spinach*!'

'Seems to like that stuff, doesn't it,' Angie said.

'Like it never tasted anything as good,' I said, drying my face on my own shirt. I was having some trouble keeping my feet and elbows still. They go a bit wild when I get agitated or upset, or if I'm taken by surprise like just now. That's where my name comes from. I jig, therefore I'm Jiggy.

When Steff's lip was licked clean, the creature's little hands felt around the rim of her nostrils and peered up them in case there was more gourmet stuff hanging around in the dark.

'Get a stick,' said Pete. 'Knock it off.'

The only sticks were on the Midden, among greasy food containers, disposable nappies, and other things I didn't want to think about.

45

'You get a stick,' I said. 'You knock it off.'

'Leave it,' Steff said. 'It only wants to be friends.'

'Friends?' said Pete. 'It lives in a rubbish dump. It's filthy.'

'Dirt can come off.'

'You're talking to the wrong boy,' Angie said. 'You want to see his feet.'

'She doesn't,' I said.

We might have expected the little creature to drop off Steff's face and bounce back to the Midden now that it had feasted, but it didn't. Perhaps it knew that if it hung around her long enough another snack would come dribbling down. It looked about for something to park on while it waited, and when it saw her nan's seed pod round her neck its eyes lit up like it had found the seat it had been looking for all its life. It swung down from her face and perched on the pod. The pod was much too small for it, but the creature didn't seem to have any trouble staying on. Steff had to keep her chin up now, right up, and couldn't move her head too easily. But she didn't seem to mind.

46

'Listen,' Angie said, leaning closer. 'It's . . .'

'Humming,' said Steff with a fond smile.

There was no tune, but the happy little mmm-ing sound was definitely sort of hummy, and then, as it sat there on the seed pod the little creature closed its eyes and the hum turned into a sort of snore.

'Think it's asleep,' I said.

'Good,' said Pete. 'Here's our chance to club it to death.'

'Don't you dare,' Steff warned.

'You can't seriously want that thing hanging around your neck and licking your face whenever your nose runs,' he said.

'It's company,' she said, stroking it.

The creature smiled in its sleep.

'What are you going to do with it?' I asked her.

'Take it home, I s'pose.'

'You're going to keep it?'

'Why not? If it'll stay.'

'You'll need a cage for it.'

'Oh, I couldn't put it in a cage.'

'It could be dangerous. It's an

unknown species.'

'It's not dangerous. It likes me.'

'Likes your snot,' said Pete.

'Well, plenty more where that came from.'

'We ought to give it a name,' said Angie.

'A name?' said Steff.

'Everyone should have a name,' said Ange.

'How about Snot of the Dump?' said Pete.

'I've got a better one,' I said.

'You would have,' he muttered.

'The Psnottead,' I said.

'The Whaty-ad?' said Angie.

'The Psnottead. The "P" is silent.'

'What "P"?'

'The silent one.'

'The Snottle,' said Steff.

'Eh?' said someone else.

'That's what we'll call it. The Snottle.'

'Best one so far,' Angie said.

'I don't know about that,' said Pete.

'Me neither,' I said.

But the Snottle it was. The women had spoken.

48

When we put the Midden behind us, the Snottle rode on the seedpod round Steff's neck like it was its own special snottle-seat.

'How does it stay on there?' Pete said. 'It's so much bigger than the pod.'

'Might have a sucker on its behind,' Steff said. 'It has some on its fingers. That's how it managed to hang on to my face.'

I felt a hand on my arm. Angie, wanting to tell me something in private. We fell back.

'Pete didn't see,' she whispered, 'probably because he has the sensitivity of a roof tile. But I did.'

'See what?'

'The future. In the nose gunge all over your face just before the Snottle licked it off.'

'Oh yes?' I still didn't believe in Future Snot, to tell you the truth. 'What did you see?'

She was just going to tell me what she thought she'd seen when a breakaway group of seagulls changed direction and dropped a week's business apiece, one after the other,

49

into my hair. Just mine, no one else's.

'That,' said Ange, scooting ahead to join the others.

CHAPTER SEVEN

Steff's house was about half a brick's throw from Borderline Way, where Pete and Angie and I lived before we moved to the Brook Farm Estate. There wasn't much of the old street left now. All but three of the houses had been demolished for redevelopment. Kind of sad to see the street where we grew up looking like that, I thought, but Pete said that he'd never seen it looking so good.

Steff's road was called Cod Row, which made me laugh because this powerful smell of fish whacked us as we turned into it. But then she pointed to this big dark building down the far end and said, 'Fish factory,' and I got it. Quite a few cats had got it too. They were mincing up and down, swishing their tails, hoping to catch a flying fin or fishy head. I thought of Stallone. Stallone's our cat. Stallone is not a gentle mog. If Stallone knew about Cod Row, his fur would be a blur. Not

51

for the fish. For all those cats to fight.

'Can't be much fun living next-door to a fish factory,' I said.

'Not quite next-door,' Steff said, stopping at the second house after the corner.

'How can you stand the smell?' Pete asked.

'We like fish.'

Suddenly there was the frantic *bee-bee-bee-bee* of a large truck reversing. We stepped on to the pavement to avoid being turned into alternative cat food.

'Fresh consignment,' Steff said, sticking her key in the lock. 'They deliver it in these manky old trucks, process it down there in that manky old factory, and next thing you know we're buying it in flash packets marked Superior Fish at the supermarket.'

She'd been cradling the Snottle with her hand to make sure it didn't fall off the seed pod, and covering it with both hands when people came near so they wouldn't see it. It had dozed most of the way to her house, but the noise of the reversing truck had woken it. It

stared through her fingers, half terrified. As Steff opened her door the frantic *bee-bee-bee-bee* stopped and the truck died. Died as in conked out. There of all places, right on her doorstep. The driver said a very fishy word and turned the engine over a few times, but it wouldn't start. We must all have had the same vision of being asked to push the truck down the street to the factory, because there was quite a scramble around the door until we were all on the other side of it.

Number 3, Cod Row wasn't a big house, but it was very bright. There were these colourful shawls and tapestry-type things on the walls, and there were fans and ostrich feathers, and wacky lampshades, and big shiny pots stuffed with grasses and stuff.

'My mum's a potter,' Steff said.

'Potty?' said Pete, as you might expect.

'Potter,' said Steff. 'Well, she *was*, but there was a slump and she couldn't keep going, and now she teaches part-time at the arts centre.'

'What'll she think of the Snottle?'

Angie asked.

'Hey, that rhymes!' said Pete. 'What'll she think of the Snottle, what'll she think of the Snottle!'

'I don't know,' said Steff. 'We don't have pets. Mum doesn't think people should own other living things. She won't turn it out, though. Wouldn't want it to suffer. Maybe she'll let me keep it, if I tell her it's a guest, not a pet.'

Her nose was running again. The Snottle's tongue reached up and licked her lip. Then it stuck one hand to her cheek and hauled itself up to scoop out her nostrils with the other. Steff giggled.

'You really don't mind that?' I asked.

'No. It's funny.'

'Might be an idea to give it a wash,' Angie said. 'No telling how long it's been in the Midden.'

Steff pulled the Snottle off her face. 'Would you like us to give you a wash then, little Snottle?' she said to it.

The creature gave a sort of squeak, then a sort of whistle, and bounced up and down excitedly in her hands.

54

'Seems to understand,' I said.

'Probably just likes being spoken to nicely,' Angie said.

'Bathroom,' said Steff.

We single-filed up a narrow staircase to the bathroom, the first room at the top. It was pretty small and the first really tatty room we'd seen there. Polystyrene tiles drooping from the ceiling, towel rail hung off, cold tap dripping, toilet-seat lid standing against the wall, doing no good at all.

'Needs redecorating,' Steff said.

I shoved my hair under a tap to shift the Seagull Gel for Boys, but maybe I didn't get it all because when I stood up, something white slithered past my right eye from my right eyebrow. I would have checked the features in a mirror, but there wasn't one. I didn't like to ask to use one of the towels and just stood about, drying off the natural way.

Steff leaned over to put the plug in the bath and turn the taps on, holding the Snottle to her neck with one hand so it wouldn't fall in. But when the water started shooting out of the taps it

panicked and scampered round the back of her neck and stared past her head at the bath, going '*Krikka-krikka-krikka*,' over and over, very fast.

'Don't expect it's ever seen a bath before,' Angie said.

'Must have,' said Pete. 'There were at least four on the Midden.'

'Do you think I should put some nice-smelling bubbly stuff in?' Steff asked us.

'It might like that,' said Ange.

Steff splashed some nice-smelling bubbly stuff in and the Snottle sat behind her head staring at the rising bubbles with eyes like mini-discs. When the bath was a quarter full, Steff tested the water with her elbow. 'My aunty does this,' she said. 'She just had a new baby.'

'Bet she's relieved she didn't have an old one,' said Pete.

Steff reached behind her neck. 'Come on, Snottle, bath time.'

The Snottle groped for her nostrils in passing, but she managed to get it off, talking gently, coaxing, and lowered it towards the water. When it

56

saw where it was going, the Snottle opened its mouth and gave a shriek like a PE teacher's whistle, which made Steff jump so much that she dropped it. There was a splash, then a lot more splashing, and more screeching from the Snottle, and then it was bobbing about making unhappy wailing sounds.

'Doesn't seem too keen on water,' I said.

'Well spotted, Jig,' said Angie.

You might expect that after the first shock the Snottle would get used to the water and the bubbles and start enjoying itself, but it didn't stick around in there long enough. It leapt out, out and up, straight up, all bubbly, hit the ceiling, and bounced around the room, smacking the walls, the floor, the ceiling again, the floor, and . . .

'Oh no!'

The last bounce had ended in the toilet.

I was nearest to the bowl and looked in. The Snottle was spluttering about like a mad thing down there. Pete appeared at my side.

'Get out of this, horror!' he cried,

gripping the flusher.

'Pete, no!' Angie yelled.

Pete gave a maniacal laugh and jerked the handle. Angie and Steff's heads joined ours over the lavvy pan. Steff reached down to try and save the Snottle, but she was too late. It span round and round in the swirling water, and with one last screech and a gurgle, hurtled off to meet its destiny on the other side of the U-bend.

58

CHAPTER EIGHT

'Garrett, you rancid scumbag!' Angie cried.

Pete was already at the door, and she would have gone after him and flushed him after the Snottle, but . . .

'Uh-uh-uh-uh-uh-uhwaaaaa!'

After a wail of misery, Steff had burst into tears. So instead of flushing Pete, Angie shoved her arms round her. Unfortunately, when she did this she trapped Steff's own arms, which stopped her lifting her hands to her face to cut off the snonk that only she knew was coming. She did manage to turn her head to one side, though, which was nice of her because it meant that she snonked over the tiles above the washbasin instead of one of us.

I was the first to see that there was something in the thick green stuff bubbling down the tiles. I looked closer. And . . .

'There *are* pictures in it!'

'Apologies accepted,' Angie said.

'But only the grovelling I'll-be-your-slave-forever-for-not-believing-you kind.'

'Look!' I said. 'There's Pete!'

Angie looked. And laughed. ' 'Xactly what he deserves.'

'What is it?' Pete said from the door.

'It's what's going to happen to you,' I said. 'Oh boy.'

He covered his ears. 'I don't want to hear!' He shut his eyes. 'I don't want to see!'

'I thought you didn't believe the pictures-in-the-snot thing,' Angie said.

'What?' he said, uncovering his ears and opening one eye.

'I said I thought you didn't believe the pictures-in-the-snot thing.'

'I don't. But I still don't want to know what you think you see.'

He started to leave.

'Where you going?' I asked.

'Home, where people don't snonk on things and nothing ever happens.'

'Are you sure you want to go out there?'

'Try and stop me!'

He left. We heard him jumping down

60

the stairs, four at a time.

'We ought to tell him,' I said to Angie.

'Don't you dare,' she said. 'The little toe-rag deserves this after what he just did.'

She turned to Steff, sitting on the side of the bath sniffing into her hands, saying, 'Snottle, Snottle, poor little Snottle,' stuff like that. She hadn't even bothered to wipe the tiles, and they looked pretty nasty, I can tell you. The pictures had disappeared though.

'Is there a window overlooking the street?' Angie asked her.

'My mum's room, just across the landing.'

Ange and I dashed to her mother's room, and opened the window. The fishy smell of the truck below hit us. The truck was still in conk-out mode, with the driver fiercely slapping the controls, hoping one of them would work if he treated it badly enough. The last control he slapped was one he shouldn't have touched this side of the factory at the end of the street, but he was annoyed and would have hit

61

anything just to make himself feel better. And this control did work. It was the one that activated the tippy-tip part of the truck. It tipped up, the tailgate flapped open, and a tidal wave of dead fish started slithering down a split second after the front door opened and Pete left the house. He trod on a stray cod, or it could have been a haddock, I don't know, and his legs flew out from under him. Next thing he knew, he was flat on his back in the street and fish were raining down on him from the truck. All he had time to say before he disappeared from sight was 'Wha—?!' Hard to beat for a famous last word.

Until then, there'd been just a handful of hungry cats sauntering along the street peering in the gutters. But when the truck plonked its load, there were masses of them, all in a flash, coming from every direction, and jumping on the fish mountain. Pete's head shot out the top like a sudden weed. There was a fish in his mouth. A cat darted at him and started pulling at it, and Pete—why, I'll never know—

held on, wouldn't let go, so that a tug-o-war started. When he finally realised what he was doing, he let the cat have the fish. The cat tumbled backwards, fish in jaws, and other cats piled on to it, tried to get the fish away from it, even though there were a million others, all staring back at them, within reach of claw and whisker.

Pete heard our chortling and, spitting fins and scales, looked up at the window.

'This is what we saw in the Future Snot!' I shouted down.

'Believe it *now*, Garrett?' said Angie.

CHAPTER NINE

Next morning at breakfast my mother had one of her twice-weekly goes at Dad about his waistline. Usually he doesn't listen, just opens the Daily Thing, which he says he buys for the sport, fooling no one. 'Mel, I can't see your belt any more when you sit down,' she said.

'Do you want to?' he said, turning to his favourite page.

'You really ought to join a gym, you know.'

'You can talk,' he said, ogling the colossal pair of boobs before him. [On the page.]

'Me?' my mother said. 'I'm in very good shape for my age.'

'What age is it today, then?'

'Are you saying that I'm losing my figure?'

'Wouldn't dare,' said Dad, turning the boobs on their side for a worm's eye view.

'You can be very cutting,' Mum said.

'And you can't?'

'I wasn't trying to be insulting, I was just stating a fact.'

'Tell you what,' Dad said. 'I'll leave your shape alone if you'll leave mine. Deal?'

'You don't have a shape,' said Mum.

'So I'm overweight? That what you're saying?'

'I wouldn't be so unkind. I'm sure it's pure coincidence that when someone says the words "tub of lard" you come to mind.'

'Right, that's it!' Dad said, chucking the paper in the air and leaping after it. 'You've insulted me for the last time.'

'Oh dear,' Mum replied. 'What will I do for fun now?'

Ten minutes later, as I was coming out of the bathroom, I found my father checking himself sideways in the full-length mirror on the landing. He was stripped to the waist (top half), experimenting with the natural look (breathing out) and the unnatural one (chest round his ears).

'Do you think I'm putting it on, Jig?' he asked.

'Scuse me,' I said. 'I can't get by.'

*   *   *

It's pretty sad when the most interesting thing you can think of to say about school is that the decorators are in, but that's the way it was that week. They'd started at half-term but not finished yet, and we were told not to get in their way or stand gawping at them. A couple of them were on a plank between two stepladders outside Mr Hurley's when we got there for History.

History teachers are obsessed with things that aren't there any more. They live in the past and expect us to want to live there too. I can't imagine that any history lesson can be a thrill a minute, but with Mr Hurley in command the expression 'To die for' takes on a whole new meaning. Mostly we sit there sighing and thinking, 'Why are the clock hands moving so slowly, has the battery committed suicide?' Mr Hurley is a very boring teacher. I mean *very* boring. He looks boring and

66

sounds boring and everything he says *is* boring. He is Mr Boring-Boring, Sir Boringest, Lord Boring of Boring-in-the-Brain. He drones on and on and on about nothing you want to know, then writes it all on the blackboard and tells us to copy it down, or write an essay on it, or ask him questions. He doesn't get many questions, mainly because no one's been listening or trying to read his crabby handwriting. There was only one time he got our attention in one of his lessons, and that was *because* we weren't paying attention. There we were, dozing on our arms, when he said something that made at least fifteen pairs of eyelids jump up like they had rockets under them.

'What did he say?' I whispered to Pete.

'Pubic Wars,' he whispered back in disbelief.

I looked around. Half the class—the boy half—was leaning forward and for the first time ever, listening, I mean really *listening*, to Hurley Twaddle.

'Wot's a Pubic War, Jig?' Eejit Atkins whispered over my shoulder.

'Why don't we shut up and find out?' I said.

'Maybe he'll do a drawin' for us to copy,' he said hopefully.

But it didn't take us long to find out that we'd heard wrong, that the word was 'Punic'. Then we rushed back to sleep to stop ourselves getting the faintest idea what a Punic War was.

Today was the first time Snonking Steff had been in Mr Hurley's class. He must have wanted to show her who was boss from the word go because five minutes into the lesson, he shuffled over to her desk, where she was sniff-sniff-sniffing non-stop, and looked down at her.

'Steffany, isn't it?' he said.

'Yes, sir.'

'Well Steffany, have you been told that you're not supposed to wear jewellery in school?'

'Um . . . not sure, sir.'

'Well you're not. And necklaces constitute jewellery.'

She fingered the seed pod round her neck. 'This isn't a necklace, sir, it belonged to my nan. Sort of a lucky

68

charm.'

'It might be a lucky charm to you, Steffany, but to the school it's jewellery, so remove it please.'

Steff wasn't the kind of girl to argue with a man as serious as Mr Hurley. She undid the shoelace and dropped the pod in his palm. He told her that he would return it at the end of the lesson and that she wasn't to wear it to school again. Steff sighed unhappily. She'd already been depressed without this. She missed the Snottle and wouldn't even *look* at Pete, the murdering little flusher.

Mr H must have liked the feel of the pod because when he went back to his desk, he didn't put it down. He tossed it up and down in one hand while the other was writing fascinating stuff about Doric Columns, whatever they are, on the blackboard. He'd been banging on about these things for seventeen and a half minutes before he had that little word with Snonker. I knew it was seventeen and a half minutes because I'd timed him to try and make the lesson more interesting.

I'd failed, but at least I'd managed to miss every word. So had everybody else from the look of them. Even those who were pretending to copy down all the guff on the board were actually doodling or writing notes in capitals to pass round. Hurley didn't notice that his class had died of boredom. He never does. He can see a necklace on the other side of the room, but when people go into rigor mortis all round him, he keeps going right on without a pause.

But something did get through to him in the end. He stopped writing. Stopped tossing the pod. Turned round. His nose was running, I noticed.

'What's that dreadful smell?' he demanded.

'What dreadful smell, siiiiir???' said a batch of voices.

'*That* dreadful smell,' he snapped.

'WHAT DREADFUL SMELL, SIIIIIR???' said the batch plus seven or eight more, at full volume.

But some of us, those nearest the windows, had smelt it too. Smells are pretty common in our class and there's

always someone you try and blame them on, but this was ten times worse than the usual classroom pong. It was like a sewer. Not that I've ever been down a sewer, you understand.

'Open the windows!' Hurley commanded with a mighty sniff.

A couple of the windows were already open a bit, but now we had an excuse to leap up and run across the top of the desks and open the rest too, then bang them shut, open them again, and bang them shut again before finally shoving them so wide they almost came off their hinges.

'Quiet, you people!!!'

We returned to our seats as quietly as we could (like an army of old-time warriors on tiptoe) and settled down. Slowly.

'Now, where was I?' Mr H sniffed, turning to the blackboard.

'You were just going to say we could go early,' said Bryan Ryan.

'Thank you, Ryan. Ah yes . . .'

He added some more scribbles to the board. He certainly had a lot to say about Doric Columns. The way things

were going, though, by the end of the lesson he would still be the only person in the room who knew whether the things were made *of* Doric, *in* Doric, *by* Doric, or *for* Doric. Still, it was quite comforting to know that so little had happened since the dawn of time that he thought we ought to know about things that prop up buildings. Hate to feel we were missing something.

Gradually, in spite of the amazing things he was writing on the board, Mr Hurley noticed that the dreadful smell was still with us. In fact, it was roughly twelve and a quarter times more dreadful now.

'Where is it *coming* from?' he said, jiggling Steff's seed pod in his hand and sniffing like crazy.

'It's comin' from aahtside, sir!' shouted Eejit Atkins.

'Well, we'd better close the windows then, hadn't w—' He stopped, realising what this would mean. 'No, *I'd* better close them.'

He started leaning over desks, one after the other, to close the windows. The smell was getting worse by the

72

minute, and naturally when he leaned over and showed us his shiny rear end we decided to look no further. He heard our snickers.

'What are you all laughing at?' he said, glaring over his shoulder. Strings of green liquorice swung from his nostrils and decorated his shoulder pad. The handful of snickers became a class-wide guffaw. 'I SAID WHAT ARE YOU LAUGHING AT???' Hurley bawled.

'It's National Laughter Day, sir,' said one boy.

'It's no such thing, Jennings. Now be quiet, all of you!'

'Want to borrow my hanky?' someone else asked.

'I said be *quiet*!' Hurley flipped back to the window—and found something unexpected staring at him.

'Snottle!' cried Steff, seeing it too.

And there it sat, on the ledge, eyeing the leaky Hurley beak. The Snottle had brought the stink with it from the Land of U-Bend.

Hurley backed away from the still-open window with bulging eyes. The

Snottle bounced in.

'Here, Snottle,' Steff said to it.

But it didn't go to her. It sprang past her, bounced off a desk, and became a growth on the Hurley phizog. He gave a muffled shout as the Snottle snaffled the hanging stuff. Steff's seed pod fell from his hand as Hurley staggered backwards trying to tear the Snottle off his face. You may not be surprised to hear that the class was pretty much in uproar by this time.

It can't have been much of a meal for a hungry Snottle. In no time it was running its little fingers around the rims of the hairy Hurley nose holes, so as not to miss a single delicious drop. Mr H staggered blindly about while his schnozzle was being milked, but he came to a halt when the Snottle, with a single bound, swapped his face for the seed pod on his desk. Once parked, the Creature of the Midden's eyes went all heavy and it started up with this chirrupy-churrupy contented sort of sound. It didn't seem to notice the racket all about it, or the kids edging closer and closer, very cautiously, for a

74

better look at it.

The history honcho didn't seem to know whether to be horrified, scared or angry about all that had just happened to him, but as he was Mr Hurley he went with angry, snatched up a metal ruler, and crept up behind the Snottle. Steff saw this, and was just rushing to the rescue of her new friend when Hurley threw his head back and snonked with the force of an H-bomb. [Hurley bomb.] More nose juice than you ever saw leave a person's muzzle in one go splashed against the blackboard, spread across it, and started down it taking all the truly fascinating guff about Doric Columns with it.

Well, the Snottle wasn't the sort of beastie to refuse seconds. It leapt off the pod, suckered itself to the board, and tucked in, lapping this way and that and above and below before the stuff could even *think* of drying up and flaking off. There was a lot of shouting and desk-walking going on at this time, so I might have been the only one to see the moving picture on the board a moment before the Snottle licked it off. 'Oh-ho,' I said. If it hadn't been Mr Hurley I might have warned him not to leave the room just yet, but it was, so I didn't. He was already lurching out of the room anyway.

KERRRRRRRASH!!!

Kids trampled over one another to get to the door and see what had happened in the corridor. I didn't. I stayed at my desk. I didn't need a rerun. I'd already seen Mr Hurley trip over one of the painters' ladders, and the enormous tin of paint topple off the wobbling plank as he went down, turning him in a trice into the only blue history teacher on Earth. I'm not a huge slapstick fan as a rule, but it really hit the spot this time.

CHAPTER TEN

Steff grabbed her dead nan's seed pod and necked it again. Now that he'd licked the blackboard clean, the Snottle seemed glad to see her, and she was glad to have him back. He looked pretty disgusting, though, and stank the classroom out, so she bundled him up in a jacket that hung over one of the chairs—Ryan's, my choice—and headed for the girls' toilets with Angie.

'He wasn't too happy last time you tried to wash him,' I reminded her, following with Pete.

'We'll just wipe him down this time,' she said.

'How come it's suddenly a him?' said Pete.

'How would you like to be called an it?' said Angie.

'He already is,' I muttered.

While Angie and Steff smuggled the Snottle into the Girls', Pete and I hung around near the door. Not too near. The odd kid and even odder teacher

77

passed every now and then, but nobody asked why we were standing there, which was a relief.

When they came out a few minutes later, Steff was carrying the Snottle wrapped up in her huge hanky. One snottlish eye peeked out.

'How was it this time?' I asked.

'Easy-peasy,' Angie said. 'I held him while Steff dabbed him clean, and he made these sweet little burbling noises. Seemed to enjoy it.'

'Where's Ryan's coat?'

'Hung it on a hook in one of the cubicles. Think we should take it back to him?'

'Absolutely not.' I'm not Bry-Ry's biggest fan.

The bell had gone at some point between Hurley turning blue and the Snottle-wash, but before shuffling out to the playground we went to the classroom for our gear. Ryan was there, looking puzzled.

'Anyone seen my jacket?'

'No.'

'No.'

'No.'

'What jacket?'

Soon that jacket, which had his name in it, would be found in a girls' toilets, smelling quite a bit worse than roses, and rumours would start about Ryan. I was looking forward to passing them on.

Outside, we went to the Concrete Garden for a pow-wow. 'Funny thing,' Steff said on the way. 'I stopped sniffing for a while in class, but I started again as we headed for the Girls', and now it's as bad as ever.'

When we were sitting down—on girl benches and boy benches, Theirs and Theirs—Steff let the Snottle out of the hanky. It jumped straight on to the seed pod round her neck. It reached for a handful of its favourite nosh and scooped it into its mouth.

'That pod,' Angie said to Steff. 'Do you take it off at night?'

'Course. Too big to keep on in bed. Why?'

'Do you snonk in the night? And does your nose run?'

'Not so far as I know, but I'm asleep.'

'Well is your pillow all snotty when you wake up?'

'Um . . . no.'

'So you probably don't.'

Steff's eyes went very wide. A bubble appeared at her left nostril and might have burst if a snottlish little finger hadn't got to it first.

'You think . . . ?'

'Let's look at the evidence,' Angie said, suddenly a big-time lawyer explaining stuff to a jury. 'You don't sniff at night after you've taken the pod off, you stop sniffing when Hurley takes the pod away from you, and he starts sniffing instead, and when the pod is right by him on his desk . . . ?'

'*He* snonks,' Steff said.

'Right. And when the Snottle bounced in the classroom window, it didn't go to you, it went to Hurley—whose nose was running.'

'So what you're saying . . .'

'Is that it's the seed pod that makes you sniff and snonk, not something in the air, not some mysterious allergy. The pod. Be the same for anyone wearing it, touching it, standing really

80

close to it. First they get the nose-runs, then they snonk.'

'And all this time . . .' Steff murmured.

'Now we know why your nan only snonked when she was working. It was the only time she wore the pod.'

'What about the pictures in the snot?' I asked.

'Must come with the allergy,' Angie said.

'You said it wasn't an allergy,' said Steff.

'Can't think of another word. And it must be a *kind* of allergy. Something in the pod that causes this reaction in people.'

'So Steff's nan wasn't clairvoyant after all,' I said.

'Oh,' said Steff. 'Oh, that's right. If it was the pod . . .' She sounded quite disappointed.

'Any idea where the old girl got it?' Pete asked. First time he'd spoken since we sat down.

Steff shook her head. 'Probably somewhere round here. Nan only started telling fortunes after she moved

81

here, Mum said. Long time ago. When Mum was little.'

'It doesn't matter where she got it,' I said. 'What matters is that now you know what causes the snonking and sniffing all you have to do to stop is take the pod off.'

'What about the Snottle?' she said.

'What about him?'

'Well, if I don't wear the pod, my nose'll stop running and he'll probably go away. I don't want to lose him. I love him.'

'Bless,' said Angie with a sugary smile.

'Someone could turn this into a musical,' said Pete.

'Musical?' I said.

'The Sound of Mucus.'

What happened next couldn't have been better timed. Or aimed. Pete was sitting there with his school bag on his knees when Steff gave a little gasp and started struggling to get her hanky out of her sleeve. As usual she wasn't fast enough. When she snonked she didn't do it in the hanky as planned. She did it over . . .

'My bag!' Pete cried.

He threw the bag to the ground in disgust. Steff started apologising like mad, but the Snottle soon put a stop to that by jumping up and getting to work on her nose. I leaned over Pete's bag to see if there were any moving pictures on it. There were. And I was in them. So was Pete, and he was doing something I wouldn't be happy about.

I jumped up. Suddenly my feet wanted to dance. Not in a bright, happy sort of way. More like a soft-shoe shuffle over a cliff.

'What's your problem?' Angie wanted to know.

'Him,' I said, thumping Pete. He fell off the bench.

'What was that for?'

Out of the corner of my eye, I saw the Snottle bounce on to his bag and start licking.

'It's for what you'll do to me given half a chance,' I said.

'What are you talking about?'

'Never mind. Don't even think about it, that's all.'

'Think about what?'

83

'Stay away from me, Garrett. Don't come near me till I say. Got it?'

'You're crazy,' he said, snatching the bag by the snot-free strap. The Snottle fell off and bounced back to Steff. Pete loped off, holding the bag as far away from him as he could.

Angie cottoned on. She asked what I'd seen in the Future Snot.

'This is one I'm keeping to myself,' I said.

'Why?'

'Because if it gets about and Pete hears, he'll do what I've seen him do in the Future Snot, and that means I'd have to hunt him down with something heavy, like a tank, and flatten him mercilessly.'

84

CHAPTER ELEVEN

It was almost teatime at *The Dorks*. *The Dorks* is the name of our house. Why *The Dorks*? I don't want to talk about it. [Well if you must know, it was my fault. But how was I to know that my parents, for once in their ancient lives, would do something I suggested? For the full fascinating story read *The Poltergoose*. (Though personally I wouldn't bother.)] When I say it was almost teatime, I mean tea should have been along any minute. In fact, it was late. I hadn't eaten a thing for at least an hour and my stomach had started complaining. My father and I were in the living room waiting for the shout from the kitchen. I was on my knees at the coffee table working on *Captain Neasden, Superprat*, and Dad was on his bot, staring at the telly. The telly still wasn't working, but he didn't seem to need an actual picture and actual sound. The earliest anyone could come and fix it was tomorrow morning, it seemed. He could live with that, just about, but it had to be working by tomorrow afternoon because it was Saturday tomorrow and Saturday afternoon means football on the box, when everyone goes out except him because he's insane.

'Jig,' Dad said suddenly. 'Do you think I ought to lose weight? I mean seriously?'

'Don't know about you,' I said, 'but I'm going to if my mother doesn't get something on that table PDQ.'

When I heard her slip into the toilet along the hall, I hoofed it to the kitchen and grabbed the jar of Hazelnut and Chocolate Spread she'd hidden behind the garlic powder and mixed herbs so I wouldn't find it. I was just dipping my fingers into the jar when a voice said:

'Ha!'

'Yipppp!' I cried as my head cracked the ceiling.

It was my mother. Instead of being in the khazi she'd become part of the wall behind the door to catch me in the act of trying not to starve. Parents. So

sly.

'I thought I'd told you not to do that,' she said.

'That was jam,' I said.

'It's everything with a lid on. Besides, you'll spoil your appetite.'

'Spoil it? I'm trying to keep my appetite from losing the will to live. Are we ever going to eat again in this house or is that it, experiment over?'

She snatched the jar of H. & Ch. Spr. from me and screwed the lid on so tight that no one would ever be able to open it again.

'It's my evening-class night,' she said.

'Don't hurry back on my account,' I said.

'I was trying to do something quick and I thought a pie, but it's taking longer than expected. Should take forty minutes, according to the instructions. It's been fifty already, and it's still not cooked.'

'What sort of pie?'

She hid the Hazelnut and Chocolate Spread again, in a different place, as if I wasn't there. 'Can't remember, look in the waste bin.'

'You're cooking it in the waste bin?'

I looked in the bin. The empty box informed me, in French, German, Urdu, Japanese and Gibberish, that we should have been tucking into Beef and Mushroom Pie by now.

'Jiggy, we're out of salt,' Mum said. 'Go across to Audrey's for some, will you? I rang her earlier, meant to go myself, but if I go now I'll never get away.'

'I don't use salt,' I said. 'Nor do you, much.'

'It's for your father. You know he can't eat anything without salt. He'll complain all through the meal if he can't put a fresh layer on every other mouthful. It'll kill him in the end. Go and get some.'

'I don't want to go over there.'

She frowned at me in that way she has, with invisible subtitles like DO AS I ASK OR I WILL GO INTO A SULK AND NOT SPEAK TO YOU FOR A WEEK. You might think that a silent mother is just what the quack ordered, but my old lady's sulks aren't like normal people's. They hang from the

88

ceiling like spears of ice. They turn the house into a tomb. Nothing dares make a sound, even a floorboard. The atmosphere is like Pompeii just after the volcano covered everything in lather.

'Why don't I go next door and borrow some from Janet instead?'

'Because Janet uses ordinary table salt and Audrey uses sea salt, same as us.'

'Dad won't know.'

'But I will. Go on now.'

'Why can't Audrey bring it here?'

'Because we're the ones who want it.'

'What are friends for if they can't bring salt when you're trying to kill your husband?'

'Jiggy, please.'

'Need to make a call first.'

'Oh! Whenever I ask you to do the smallest thing!'

I left the kitchen and snatched the hall phone. I took it to the little room where my mother should be right now with her knickers round her ankles instead of jumping out at me from walls and ordering salt. I punched

89

buttons. I put the receiver to my ear and mouth. I waited. I spoke.

'Ange. Me. I'm coming over for salt.'

'I know,' she said. 'It's in all the papers.'

'Is Pete there?'

'What do you want Pete for?'

'I don't want Pete. That's why I'm ringing you. I need you to lock him up and throw away the key till I've been and gone.'

'I think I heard him go out,' she said.

'Brilliant. Be right over then. Tell your ma to have the salt ready. Can't hang about in case the toe-rag comes back.'

I reached the Mint-Garrett residence about a minute later and rang the plastic doorbell. While waiting for the door to open, I glanced up at Pete's window. He might be out, but that window made me nervous. I hit the plastic again. No one leapt to the door, but there was movement in the kitchen to my left. Then Audrey Mint was peering through a gap in the blinds.

'Has no one let you in?!' she shouted

through the glass.

'Yes!' I shouted back. 'That's why I'm still standing on the step!'

'I'll get the salt!' she hollered.

'Wonderful!' I bawled.

As the slats of the blind closed with a slap, I heard a window opening. I looked up. It was Pete's window. I saw the rim of a pink plastic bucket tip over. I saw water gush from it. *Whooosh*! I felt the water. A whole bucketful. I blinked up through drowning eyelashes. Saw a grin flash over the ledge above.

'Hi, Jig.'

'Angie said you were out,' I said.

'Angie was wrong.'

'I'm soaked. Head to foot.'

'That's for thumping me.'

'I thumped you *because* you were going to do this.'

'You expect me to believe that you saw this in the Future Snot?'

'It's as true as I drip here.'

He was laughing as he closed the window. The front door opened. Angie looked me up and down, mostly down.

'You're all wet,' she said.

91

'Mm,' I said. 'Care to tell me why you didn't answer the door?'

'Steff phoned just after you did with a Snottle update.'

'Which is?'

'That it seems to like her bedroom. Jig, why are you all wet?'

'Because you were wrong about Pete being out.'

She looked up at Pete's window.

'The Future Snot thing?'

I nodded. Water ran into my mouth from my hair.

Audrey appeared in the doorway with a drum of sea salt.

'It's fine,' she said.

'What is?' I said.

'The salt. As opposed to crystal. Jiggy. You're all wet.'

'He knows,' said Angie.

'Why? What happened?'

'Sudden downpour,' I said, grabbing the salt and squelching back across the road bulging in all the wrong places. When I got in, I put the salt on the kitchen table. 'It's fine,' I said.

'What is?' Mum said.

'The salt. As opposed to crystal.'

'Jiggy, why are you all wet?'

'Big puddle.'

I kicked my soggy shoes off and plodded upstairs to change. Last time I go across the road for salt.

CHAPTER TWELVE

Over tea—eventual tea—Dad read the latest free paper, which had just been twisted out of shape on the step and rammed through the letter flap. Mum hates him reading at the tea table but he still does it, probably because he knows she hates it. I've tried reading at the tea table once or twice, but unlike my father I can't handle all the nagging and the scowls and the muttering.

'Idiots,' Dad said suddenly.

'What have we done?' I said.

He held the front page of the paper up for us to see. There was a photo of the Fellowship of Ancient Rights for Trees' people, waving placards at passing motorists.

'Bloody hippies,' he said. 'Tree huggers. Anything progressive, people like these want to block it.'

'Oh, so bulldozing centuries-old woodland to make way for ugly new houses is progressive, is it?'

'We live in an ugly new house,' he

94

reminded her.

'There were no trees here, just farmland.'

'And it's all right to build on open farmland, is it?'

'Bit different from destroying an ancient wood.'

My father rustled the paper and refolded it viciously.

'I don't know why you don't join this mob, the way you think.'

'Maybe I will,' she said.

'Do,' he said.

'I might,' she said.

'If you do, you can forget about darkening my door ever again.'

'It's not your door, it's our door. Joint owners, remember?'

'Biggest mistake I ever made.'

'Big mistake letting me pay half the mortgage too? Just say the word and you can pay it all yourself.'

'Don't you have to go out?' Dad said from behind the paper.

'Mind if I finish my meal first?'

'The gypsy cookery course tonight, isn't it?'

'Gypsy?'

'Romany. Same thing.'

'Romanian, Mel. Rom-anian. God, the ignorance in this household.'

'Thanks, Mum,' I said.

She flung her fork down, jumped up, and stormed out. Then she came back, but only as far as the door, and only long enough to say, 'And you *have* put on weight. A lot of weight. Keep going at this rate and you'll be clinically obese by Christmas.'

The newspaper shook in Dad's fists, but by the time he'd lowered it to say something unpleasant in return, she'd gone again. The life had gone out of him, though. His mouth looked as if it had been sewn up with garden twine and his eyebrows were an upside-down V. My old dear sure knows how to bring a man down. She ought to teach that at her adult education college. Be a sell-out, bound to be.

After Dad and I had followed Mum's written instructions telling us how to put everything in the dishwasher PROPERLY, I headed across the road for the second time in an hour. I needed revenge or I wouldn't sleep

that night. When I rang the bell, I kept my eye on Pete's window in case he tried a repeat performance.

'Any point asking if Pete's in?' I asked when Angie opened up.

'If he's not, the TV in his room's entertaining itself.'

'Where's your mum? Where's Oliver?'

She shrugged. 'About.'

I stepped inside. The living-room door was shut, but I heard a soapy sig tune, which meant the coast was clear for Payback. I didn't know what I was going to do to him yet, but I'd think of something, probably as I was doing it. No one pours water over Jiggy McCue, especially from pink plastic.

I started upstairs. Something moved on the landing. 'Garrett,' I said, 'prepare to die.'

There was a Garretty squawk, then mad feet, and a door slammed. When I got to the top, it was obvious where he'd gone. The bathroom door was closed. People always hide in bathrooms when someone's after their blood. I hammered on the door.

97

'Come out, you lousy, stinking scumbag!'

He didn't come out. I hammered again.

'Jig . . .' Angie said from behind me.

But I wasn't going to be talked out of this.

'If you don't get your stupid bum out here right now for me to kick it round the block,' I said to the wood, 'I'm going to kick the stupid door in!'

The lock turned. I remoulded my hands so they would fit round the Garrett neck without further adjustment. The door opened a crack. The crack had an eye in it. I shoved hard, heard a satisfying thud, jumped through the gap, gripped the neck that was just the other side of it, and threw it on to the damp bathmat.

'Right!' I said. 'Now!' I said. 'Oh!' I said.

I said 'Oh!' because the neck my hands were round didn't look the way I'd expected. The face above it looked kind of different too.

'Jiggy, what . . . what . . .?' said Audrey Mint as I let go of her neck and

98

sat back on her wet stomach.

'I thought you were Pete,' I said.

'Do I *look* like Pete?'

I climbed off her. 'Dead-ringer through a closed door.'

As she got to her feet, rubbing her head where the door had cracked it, she grabbed a bath towel and covered her bits. Just in time. Another second of my best bud's female parent in her Golden Oldie birthday suit and my eyes would have shattered.

'What's this all about anyway?' Audrey asked me.

'Another time,' I said, stumbling downstairs supported by the rail.

I heard Pete laughing quietly on the landing as I went.

*   *   *

Later I was trying to break into a vacuum-sealed family pack of Kit-Kats with the kitchen scissors, the bread knife and a rolling pin when the doorbell rang. 'Pete,' I thought, dropping the task at hand and reaching for the frying pan. I don't know why I thought it would be him, but that's what I expected. I went to the door. It wasn't Pete. It was a woman in a long colourful dress with tassels. As well as the long colourful dress and tassels she wore beads, and her hair was split into two halves, in long plaits. My frying-pan arm fell to my side.

'Hi,' the woman said, with a big smile. She had very bright teeth. 'I wonder if I might speak to your parents?'

'There's only one in,' I said.

'Could I speak to her? Or him?'

'Him. DAAAAD!'

She jumped back in shock, just missing a prickly end in the rose bush.

'WHAT?' (My father bellowing from Blank TV Land.)

'SOMEONE TO SEE YOU!' I yelled back.

'TELL 'EM WE DON'T WANT ANY!'

'Are you selling something?' I asked the woman.

'Not exactly,' she said, straightening her plaits.

'SHE'S NOT SELLING ANY-

100

THING!' I screamed.

Pause while Dad took this in, before
. . .

'SHE?'

'YES! SHE!'

He came out of the living room smoothing his hair down with one hand. In his other hand he held a magazine, one of Mum's, open at *Your Life in the Stars.*

'Hello,' the woman on the step said, stretching a hand towards him (one of hers). 'Serena.'

'Serena?' Dad said, looking at the hand like he'd never seen one before.

'My name.'

'Oh.' He took the hand.

'Sorry to disturb you,' Serena said, 'but I represent the Fellowship of Ancient Rights for Trees, and we're concerned about the destruction of Ingle Woods to make way for a housing estate.'

'Unggg?' Dad said, still holding her hand.

I sighed. I'd seen this before. My father meets a female type with a face that doesn't look like a baboon's back

101

end and his tongue falls out, his knees sag, and his conversation becomes pure Teletubby.

'I'm collecting signatures,' Serena said, wrestling with his grip. 'For a petition to stop the levelling of the woodland.'

Dad managed to find a few words. Four actually.

'Where do I sign?'

She must have got her hand back eventually, because when he wandered into the kitchen a few minutes later, he didn't have it with him. 'Did you see her?' he said.

'Who?'

'The gorgeous woman on the step. Wow.'

His eyes had misted over. His mind flickered behind them like an old black and white film. He was imagining himself skipping through a meadow stuffed with wild flowers, hand in mitt with the latest love of his life, singing 'We Shall Overcome' and 'Imagine' to a Golden Oldie disco beat.

CHAPTER THIRTEEN

Saturday morning. Mum and Dad up before me as usual. When I went down, there was no sign of either of them. But then I heard a key in the lock and Dad came in. He had a second-hand carrier bag under his arm.

'What do you think, Jig?' he said, tilting his head. The light caught the little gold circle on his left ear. I gulped.

'An earring? You?'

'All the best people are wearing them,' he said.

'And some of the worst. You had your ear pierced?'

'Pierced? Are you mad? No, it's a clip-on.'

I nudged the carrier bag. 'What's in there, a kaftan?'

'No, they were all out. But I've got something even better. Even your mum will be impressed with this.'

'Wouldn't count on it,' I said.

'I'll go and put it on.' He moved off,

but paused. 'Where is she?'

I shrugged. 'I'm not my mother's keeper.'

He went his way and I went into the kitchen to look for something breakfasty. I was half way through a bowl of New Improved Totally Tasteless Organic Wheatflakes when he rejoined me. He was wearing the outfit from the carrier bag.

'Captain Neasden,' I breathed softly. For it was he, to the life.

My father, who never stands on his hind legs as long as there's something to sit on, was wearing a tracksuit. And not just any tracksuit. This effort was purple spandex, two sizes too big. He would have reminded me of Tinky Winky gone to seed if not for the luminous orange headband, which matched nothing this side of Jupiter.

'Well?' he said.

'I was,' I replied, looking for something to lean on.

'Is it me?'

'Exactly what I was thinking.'

'I've had it with your mother's snide remarks,' he said. 'I'm losing weight.

104

The pounds are going to fall off.'

'You don't automatically lose weight by putting on a tracksuit,' I explained.

'Of course you don't. Unfortunately. I'm taking up jogging.'

'Jogging? You?'

'Jogging. Me. Go on, laugh.'

'I'm not laughing. The country needs more joggers. Where would horizons be without them? But Dad . . . why that tracksuit? I mean, with a billion and five to choose from, why *that* one?'

'It was the only one left at Help the Aged.'

'And the unmatching headband?'

'They threw it in for free.'

*   *   *

Mum had gone next door to Janet Overton's. Dad had changed out of the tracksuit by the time she returned. 'I want to surprise her,' he said to me.

'You will,' I replied.

But he left the earring on, and even though Mum was going out of her way not to look at him because she was still off him, she couldn't miss that. She

didn't say anything, but when she ran up the stairs I wasn't sure if she was laughing, crying, or desperate for a pee. There was a clue, though. When she came down a minute later there were tears in her eyes, and every so often she stuffed her hanky in her mouth.

'Jiggy,' she said when she'd got over it, 'make no plans until after lunch.'

'Why, what happens after lunch?'

'That's up to you. Before lunch we're going shopping. To SmartSave.'

My heart burst out of my chest and nose-dived into the carpet.

'Shopping? You and me?'

'And your father.'

'The three of us? Like . . . in a Family Outing?'

'Yes, I suppose so.'

'Mother,' I said. 'I cannot—I mean *can not*—be seen food-shopping with my parents.'

'Jiggy,' she said, leaning towards me and speaking slowly, the way I do with Pete sometimes. 'I'm going shopping, and I need help.'

I leaned towards her and spoke

106

slowly back. 'You're going shopping *and* you need help?'

'I do. And you're going to give it, whether you like it or not.'

I leaned back. 'I don't see why you need me as well as Dad.'

'There's a lot to get. I need three hands to carry it all.'

'Oh well, if you only need three hands, you can manage it between you, with one of his tied behind his back.'

'I need *both* of you,' she said with a heavy glare.

'Does he know?'

'He soon will.'

She tracked him down in the kitchen, and like me he didn't seem keen. 'Can't,' he said. 'TV repair man's coming.'

'When?'

'Any minute is the plan, but he's bound to be late, they always are.'

There was a ring at the doorbell.

Dad swore.

While Mum went off to do girlie stuff like make beds and hoover things, Dad and I watched the TV repairman rip the back off the set and look inside

with a pencil torch. He twiddled something, then twiddled something else, then said he couldn't fix it on the premises.

'But it's Mindless City and Undead United today!' Dad cried. [Or something like that.]

In the end, seeing that my father was on the point of throwing himself at the carpet and beating it with his fists, the repair man offered to lend him an old set from the back of his van till ours was sorted. Dad came terrifyingly close to hugging him. The new old TV turned out to be quite a bit smaller than ours, and the picture jumped, but my father was too happy to see something on a screen—anything—to care about quality.

A little while later, Mum started rounding us up for the big shopping trip. Dad was still on his perch in front of the jumpy old TV.

'No can do,' he said. 'The match.'

'It's not on for another three hours,' Mum said.

'Two hours thirteen and a half minutes.'

'Still, time enough to accompany your wife and son to the supermarket.'

'I need to get used to this old set,' Dad said.

'Get used to it while they're kicking their stupid balls. Come on, I haven't got all day.'

And that was it. My mother had spoken. She has a lot in common with Angie, my mum. Neither of them take no for an answer. In fact, they don't take anything for an answer if it's something they don't want to hear. Must be a woman thing.

*   *   *

SmartSave, the supermarket my mother likes to go to, is on the other side of town. Because it was Saturday the entire estate had the same idea, but that was just the start. Once our car and the rest of the Brook Farm Motor Club had managed to crawl on to the main road, we were joined by every other car within a five-mile radius, and for the next hour the traffic stopped and started every few seconds like a snake with hiccups. This didn't please Dad. My father hates being stuck in traffic. Every time he was forced to stop the car he growled '******,' until Mum told him not to keep saying that in front of me.

'My life isn't worth living,' he said. 'I can't even use asterisks now.'

Eventually, we joined the SmartSave filter lane, where the traffic was at even more of a standstill. Sitting in the back, ignored by my parents (also ignoring each other most of the time), I wondered if I'd be missed if I ducked below the rear-view mirror and slipped quietly out. I mean to say, what a waste of a day, sitting in an oven on wheels waiting to buy stuff you don't want, while your life clicks by on the dashboard clock. What made it even worse was that from where we sat we could see the SmartSave car park, and there were quite a lot of spaces in it, and we couldn't get to any of them. We couldn't get to them because the ticket machine wasn't working and a geriatric in a green eyeshade was handing out the tickets instead. Handing them out

so slowly you'd think he was printing them up his sleeve with a John Bull Printing Outfit.

But eventually we got to a parking space and fell out of the car. And the first thing Mum did was rip her shopping list in half.

'Good, she's torn it up,' I said to Dad. 'We can start the six-hour journey home now.'

No such luck. She gave Dad half the list and suggested they went their separate ways. 'Don't tempt me,' Dad muttered, running an eye down his bit of list. 'Well, you can forget that for starters,' he said. 'I've told you before, I will not use recycled toilet paper. You don't know where it's been.'

'Make a pretty good guess,' I said.

Mum wrenched a couple of trolleys from the trolley tangle and rolled one at Dad. He stepped aside, but I caught it. We were about to head for the entrance when we heard chanting voices from the car park exit. Protesters. With placards.

'DON'T LET THEM DO IT! DON'T LET THEM DO IT! DON'T

LET THEM DO IT!'

'What's that about?' Dad said.

'FARTers,' I said.

'What?' said Mum.

'The Fellowship of Ancient Rights for Trees.'

'No trees here,' Dad said.

'Used to be,' said Mum.

'I don't see you boycotting the supermarket.'

'There are things here that we need.'

'And things that we don't, like recycled bog rolls.'

'I'm going to see what they have to say,' Mum said. 'See you back at the car in forty-five minutes. Maximum.' She drove her trolley in the general direction of the FARTers. General direction because one of the wheels wanted to go somewhere else entirely.

'She'll be joining them before you know it,' Dad said.

'Or signing their petition,' I said with a smirk.

He looked at me. 'You wouldn't tell.'

'Depends,' I said.

'On?'

'How soon I get a decent raise in my

pocket money.'

'Jig, I can't give you any more,' he whined. 'You've blackmailed me so often I've had to get an overdraft just to keep up with you.'

He threw his trolley into SmartSave and ran after it before I could argue.

CHAPTER FOURTEEN

I didn't take a trolley myself, or even a basket, because there's just so much self-respect a kid can sacrifice for his parents. I rolled the McCue shoulders in, hands pocketed, hoping I looked like the place was beneath me. Dad was just ahead of me, and when he stopped suddenly I ploughed into him, blowing my cool in a heartbeat. Climbing out of his back pocket, I found him frowning at his bit of list.

'Jig, what's . . . keller-eye-ak?' he asked.

'Come again?' He held the list in front of my eyes. I shook my head. 'No idea.'

'Could that be celeriac?' said another voice, not mine, not Dad's.

We turned like a pair of meerkats. It was the hippy female from last night's doorstep who Dad couldn't say no to. Seeing her again he immediately lost ten centimetres in height and drooled over his shirt.

114

'Whurrrra?' he asked as his tongue swelled to twice normal size.

She leant close to him to examine the shopping list, giving him a chance to sniff her plaits, which were coiled on top of her head today like dead snakes.

'Yes, celeriac. It's a sort of cross between swede and celery.'

'Anpeepleeadit?' my father mumbled wittily.

The woman laughed and flashed her teeth at him, dazzling a couple of passers-by who ran off to look for the revolving sunglass rack.

'It's not to everyone's taste, but I like it. Here, I'll show you.'

She cartwheeled off in the direction of the veg. Dad straightened the tie he wasn't wearing and spun his trolley after her. I trailed miserably along behind. She was waiting for us with this diseased-looking bulb thing balanced on her palm. Dad tried to look fascinated by this unfamiliar veg but I knew that all he really wanted to do was fall to the floor and lick the dust off the woman's sandals. I hung back, reworking the cool by sneering at the

115

two-for-the-price-of-one   seedless grapes.

'Well, must get on,' the woman said in a minute, swinging her beads. 'I'm supposed to be outside with the others.'

'Others?' Dad said, finally mastering two syllables.

'Didn't you see them on your way in?'

'Oh yes. Them.'

'Why don't you join us?' she said.

'Join you?' Dad answered, eyes flaring like matches.

'Here's my card. In case you fancy it.'

She whipped a small card out of the little beady purse-thing that hung from her shoulder. Dad took it and gazed lovingly at it.

'Serena,' he whispered, like someone about to break into prayer.

'And you are . . . ?' she said.

'Me?' He looked up. Blankly. 'Ah. Um . . .'

Yes, folks, my father had forgotten his name.

Serena didn't wait for it to come back to him. 'Tell me when you join

us!' As she swung away, I noticed for the first time that she didn't have a trolley or basket and wasn't carrying any shopping. Dad stood gazing after her, sniffing the celeriac she'd handed him. She was close to the exit, about half a supermarket away, when she remembered something on his list that had grabbed her attention, and bawled:

'GLAD TO SEE YOU USE RECYCLED TOILET ROLLS!'

'NEVER USE ANYTHING ELSE!' Dad bawled back.

I turned to the bananas and hid my face to give bystanders a chance to forget they'd seen me in the same reality as this man. I couldn't leave the building, much as I wanted to, because Mum would go on and on, the way she does—'typical Jiggy McCue', 'downright laziness', 'if only you'd been a girl'—all the usual. Instead, I whizzed round the corner of the cereal aisle and crashed into one of the last things I like to find my face in on a Saturday morning: the six-pack of my giant PE teacher, Mr Rice.

'Steady, son, watch where you're . . .

Well, if it isn't my old friend McCue!'

One of the troubles with Mr Rice—just one!—is that he wouldn't know how to speak quietly if you slipped him a dozen sleeping pills, dragged him by the collar into the reference section of a library, and hammered a cricket ball into his trap.

'Didn't recognise you without the stupid red tracksuit, sir,' I said.

'It's the weekend!' he boomed.

'Stupid blue jeans instead, eh?!' I boomed back.

'Exactly!'

Mr Rice in jeans took some getting used to, but I tried not to stare in case people started talking. The rest of him was pretty standard, weekend or no weekend. The face, the hair, the trainers the size of Japanese whaling boats.

'Hello, Jiggy,' said another voice, a normal one this time. 'Helping your folks with the weekly shop?'

Miss Weeks, Ranting Lane's Deputy Head. Who for some reason no one could understand had linked up with Mr Rice. Something to do with the fact

118

that they both liked sport, was the best anybody could come up with. Miss W was another female who did stuff to my father's knees and speech. If he saw her after talking celeriac with Serena he'd be a heap of Dad-flavoured jelly by the time we got him home.

'You got it, Miss. Toodle-oo!'

Shimmying round another corner, I had to swerve to miss a small podgy man in little round glasses examining tea labels. I might not have noticed him if he'd been in normal clothes, but he was wearing a green camouflage jacket and blue camouflage trousers. If he'd been lying on top of a tall tree with his legs in the air enemy planes might not have picked him off, but in SmartSave on a Saturday morning he stood out like a sore thumb. A camouflaged one.

'Hello, Jiggy.'

I slapped my forehead. This was not the place to be! I turned.

'On your own?' Steff asked.

'If only.' I nodded at the bump on her chest, under her coat. 'Snottle?'

'Yes. I think he's asleep.'

'Must be. Your nose is running.' She

119

wiped it. 'Hey, if your nose is running you must still be wearing the pod under there.'

'The Snottle likes to sit on it.'

'You could leave it at home, let him sit on it there.'

'Oh, I couldn't. He's company.'

I asked what she was doing there. Pretty stupid question in a supermarket, so I wasn't surprised when she jerked her basket at me. There wasn't much in it.

'On your own?' I said.

'Mum's busy. As ever.'

'Does she know about the Snottle yet?'

'No.'

'She hasn't noticed it under your coat?'

'I told her it was something I'm wearing for a dare. She said she's glad I'm entering into things at Ranting Lane. Edam.'

'What?'

'Dutch cheese. Need some.'

She headed for the delicatessen counter and I felt obliged to head there with her because neither of us had said

goodbye. While she was buying the Edam and I was standing there looking cool and bored, I noticed a small table at the end of the counter. It was covered with a green cloth and attended by a woman in a silly green hat and matching apron. There were all these little saucers on the table, and on each of the saucers there was a cracker with a lump of something on top. When Steff had got her Edam, she asked the woman what the lumps on the crackers on the saucers on the table were.

'Baumingthorpe Cheese,' the woman said. 'It's new. Vegetarian. Try some.'

Steff picked up a cracker. She was about to bite into it when she gave a big sniff and a small gasp—'Oh no! Snonk coming!'—and dropped the cracker.

'Snonk?' said the woman.

'Sneeze,' I told her. 'She has this allergy . . .'

Steff tried to put her hand in front of her face, but she wasn't quick enough. With a deafening honk, thick green goo burst from her nose and landed on the

demonstrator's apron and table. The apron was plastic, so it started slithering downward right away, but the tablecloth wasn't, and it stayed. It clung to the cheese and crackers, particularly the cheese, all green and glistening. Strangely, the woman seemed more bothered by the state of her apron than the table, and she rocketed through the hanging rubber flaps beside the delicatessen counter to wipe it down.

Because no one was looking when Steff snonked, there were no other witnesses. Plenty of people heard it, but by the time they decided it came from somewhere near us the nose juice had settled on the Baumingthorpe and was sinking into the cloth. Not before we saw a moving picture in it, though.

Steff said: 'It looks like . . .'

'Mr Rice,' I said as the picture drained away. 'And look what he's—'

'Who speaketh my name in vain?!' boomed a voice behind me.

'What was that noise?' Miss Weeks asked.

'The fruitcake standing next to you,' I said.

'New cheese, eh?!' bawled old Ricicles. 'Looks good! Moist, just the way I like it!'

Steff's chest heaved suddenly. The slumbering Snottle had got a whiff of elevenses. She gripped the neck of her jacket as Mr Rice took our place at the table. An enormous Rice-paw fell on a poor defenceless little cracker and popped it in his mouth. He crunched. Something green trickled down his chin.

'Excellent!' he said.

He pounced on another cracker. He swallowed that too, eyes rolling. I nodded to myself. It made sense. Rice is crackers, so he would be crackers about crackers. He'd also discovered that he was pretty partial to Baumingthorpe Cheese, as we'd known he would be from the moving picture in the Future Snot on the table. There was no holding him now. One after the other he scooped up crackers and the cheese with the secret ingredient, shovelling every ultra-moist morsel into his face. Steff and I should have vamoosed by this time, but here was a teacher eating snot-covered cheese. Besides, the Snottle was going wild inside her coat and she was struggling to keep it in. Suddenly he squeezed out. He dropped on to the table. He sucked the paper-cloth dry in two secs. Then he turned to the big lunk who'd snaffled his favourite grub.

Mr Rice was gawping at the Snottle with bulging eyes and gaping mouth. It was the gaping mouth that interested the Snottle. He jumped, and with his cute little hands held the Rice lips apart while he peered past the Rice teeth. He might have shoved his tongue in and dried out the Rice tonsils, but Mr R gripped him with both hands and flung him away as hard as he could. Unfortunately, he did this at the very moment the SmartSave manager chose to come and see what that snonking sound had been about. The Snottle smacked the manager on the forehead, and while the manager tumbled sideways into the Greek yoghurts, bounced off in the direction of Household Goods.

As Miss Weeks and a couple of other

customers helped the manager out of the yogs, and Mr Rice spluttered some unbelievable rubbish about being attacked by a green ball or vegetable with eyes, Steff and I slipped quietly away.

CHAPTER FIFTEEN

After lunch, I went over to Pete and Angie's. We sat in their kitchen while I told them what had happened in SmartSave. They loved the moist cheese almost as much as Mr Rice did.

'What happened to the Snottle?' Angie asked.

I shrugged. 'Still bouncing around Dusters and Broom Handles for all I know.'

'Wasn't Steff upset?'

'What about?'

'Losing the Snottle.'

'Dunno. She went to the cash desk and I went to the car park to wait for the Golden Oldies. Last I saw of her.'

'I've been thinking about that seed pod of hers,' Angie said. 'I think we ought to take it to the garden centre to see if they can identify it, tell us what it is.'

'Who cares what it is?' Pete said.

'Aren't you the slightest bit interested?'

126

'No.'

'Stay here then. We'll go without you.'

By 'we' she meant me, and as I had no bigger deals lined up I didn't argue. She phoned Steff's home number to invite her too. Seemed a good idea, seeing as she had the pod. There was no answer. Angie might have tried her mobile next, but she didn't have the number.

'Now what?' I said.

There was no answer to that either. A sensationally boring Saturday afternoon loomed before us. I suggested dreaming up some more rules for the Musketeer Rule Book, but Pete said we already had three, what did I want, a dictatorship?

I narrowed my eyes at him. 'There's still the little matter of revenge. Revenge could take up a fair bit of the afternoon.'

'You already did the revenge,' he said. 'In advance. There's a bruise on my shoulder the size of Finland.'

'Finland is long and thin,' said Angie.

127

'So's the bruise.'

When Mum came over to talk to Audrey about hair, we zoomed across the road to my place. Stallone was on the step. As usual, he spat at us as we stepped over him.

'Got the box on, has he, Stal?' I asked.

'Grrrr!' he said.

Stallone hates football as much as I do. But then Stallone hates everything.

The sporty Saturday-afternoon TV warm-up splatted our ears as we stepped over the threshold. Dad was already in position, sprawled on the couch in his baggy underwear, football rattle poised, crate of SmartSave Russian Lager (warm) within reach.

Pete leant in to ask who was playing. Dad told him. 'Never heard of 'em,' Pete said.

'They probably never heard of you either,' Dad said.

Cracks me up, my old man.

We went to the kitchen, where we passed the new giant bottle of SmartSave Super Cola from mouth-to-mouth until we felt like we were going

128

to whizz round the room like freed balloons.

'You know where she could be, don't you?' Angie said with a burp.

'Who?' I burped back.

'Steff,' she burped.

'Where?' I burped.

'The woods,' she burped. 'They're going to start lopping trees on Monday. Last *burp* chance *burp* to get it stopped.'

I don't know, maybe Steff was a bit psychic after all, because just then Angie's mobile rang and it was her. She'd phoned to ask if we'd seen the Snottle since SmartSave, because she was worried about him. Angie burped, said we hadn't, and asked Steff where she was. As we'd thought, she was at the woods with her mum and the other FARTers. Ange asked how the protest was going. Steff said OK, why don't you come and join us? Ange said we'd love to but we had this really heavy burp on. Then she and Pete went home because they couldn't think of any reason to stay now the cola was gone, and I toddled up to my room to carry on with

129

Captain Neasden, Superprat.
Weekends. So exciting.

*　　　*　　　*

I must have dozed off or Dad's yell wouldn't have made me jerk the way it did. I was lying on the rug beside my bed with Captain Neasden on my face. I got to my knees and shuffled to the door.

'Uuurgh?!' ['What!?'] I said.

'I'm going out!' Dad bawled from the foot of the stairs. 'If anyone wants me, I'm . . . out.'

'Uuurgh,' ['Terrific. Wonderful. Thanks for telling me. I'll pass it on to anyone who gives a monkey's.'] I said.

I got up off my knees and started downstairs on my feet. It's usually easier that way. Not this time though, because one of my legs was still asleep and I had to haul it separately, by hand. By the time I got to the bottom Dad was at the front door. He was wearing sandals and beads. Yes, sandals. Yes, beads. My father. But I didn't want to give him a complex. 'Father,' I broke it

130

to him gently. 'You look a complete prawn. Make sure you go out with a bag over your head.'

He looked down at himself. 'You don't think it's me?'

'Of course it's you, I'd know that dandruff anywhere. What about the match?'

'Match?'

'The footie.'

'Bad game. Giving it a miss.'

I staggered. 'Giving it a *miss*? You're missing a *game*? You?'

I'd never known my father to elbow a game once it started. It didn't matter who was playing or how useless they were, it had to be watched to the last gasp, last hug, last kiss around the goalmouth. And even then it wasn't over most of the time. For the next five hours he had to watch the managers and commentators, and the moronic players with their tattoos and poncy hairdos, waffling about what happened or didn't happen, who'd done what or hadn't done it, and why. Normal people would turn to dust with boredom while these things are

131

onscreen. Not football fans. Not my father. Usually.

'Where you going?' I said.

'I need some air,' he replied, kind of shiftily, I thought.

'Quite a bit of that in the garden,' I reminded him.

'Yeah, well . . . someone to see.'

'Anyone I know?'

'No.'

'Who?'

'Nobody,' he said, putting the door between us in a hurry, like I do with my mother when she starts asking awkward questions.

I went to the kitchen and flipped the lid off the biscuit-tin-I-wasn't-supposed-to-know-about in the back of the gifts-we-hate cupboard. While trying to get into the new packet of SmartSave Custard Creems with my teeth, I heard heavy breathing at my ankles. Stallone.

'Forget it, pal,' I said. 'These are secret. No one's supposed to know about them. That means you as well as me.'

I carried the packet to the window

132

and leant over the sink to watch Dad back the car out of the garage, just miss the lamppost, and putter off down the street. He'd only just made it out of sight when Mum and Audrey came out of Pete and Angie's. Mum glanced at the open garage as they strolled up the path. She said something to Audrey. I remembered that I wasn't supposed to have found the secret bickies and threw the packet back in the tin. Not before I shoved a bundle in my pocket, though. Stallone narrowed his eyes at me and swore in Catese as I slammed the cupboard door in his furry face.

'Where's your father?' Mum said as she and Audrey breezed in.

'Out,' I said.

'Well obviously *out*. The car's gone. Why isn't he watching TV?'

'Bad match.'

'That doesn't usually stop him.'

'That's what I thought.'

'Say how long he'd be?'

'No.'

She tutted. 'Now what?' she said to Aud.

'There's a bus goes that way,' Audrey

133

said. Audrey doesn't drive.

'I can't remember the last time I went anywhere by bus,' Mum said.

'It's like reality TV,' I said. 'Where you going anyway?'

'To the woods!' cried Aud, shoving a fist on her hip and pointing at the extractor fan.

'Ingle Woods to join the protesters,' said Mum, less dramatically.

'The FARTers?' I said.

'I wish you wouldn't call them that,' she said.

'They chose the name, not me. You're not serious? You're not really going to join them?'

'We've decided that it's a good cause,' Audrey said. 'There are few enough trees left around here.'

'It won't do any good,' I said. 'The land's been sold and they're crunching the wood on Monday.'

'Well informed all of a sudden, aren't we?' Mum said.

'Don't know about you,' I said, heading doorward. I was almost there when something fell out of my pocket and shattered on the phoney quarry

tiles.

Mum swooped towards the dropped Custard Creem, but Stallone saved my skin by darting under her fingers, clamping his jaws on it, and flying out of the room to scoff it before she was quite sure what it was.

When Mum and Aud left, I wandered through to the living room wondering what other fascinating things I could do with my day. I noticed that the telephone receiver wasn't on the way Mum likes it. We have one of those old-fashioned phones, which aren't old-fashioned at all, they just look it, and whenever Dad uses it he puts the receiver back the opposite way to the way Mum says it should be. I think he does it on purpose to annoy her. I was so desperate for something to do that I picked the receiver up to turn it round, like Mum would when she saw it. It was still in my hand when I thought of something even more fascinating to do: press Redial to see who'd been called last. This is ultra-boredom for you. The dialling tone started. I got ready to click off when whoever it was picked up. Suddenly there was a lot of muffled shouting in my ear.

'HANDS OFF OUR ANCIENT TREES! HANDS OFF OUR ANCIENT TREES! HANDS OFF OUR—'

Then someone was screaming into the receiver, trying to make themselves heard over the chanting.

'Hello? Hello! Serena here! You'll have to speak up!'

I dropped the receiver. It landed the right way round in the cradle. Then my feet were moving, hands twitching, as I jigged along with the full scenario tangoing past my eyes. My father, bored for the first time ever with a TV footie match, had remembered his little chat over the celeriac that morning. 'Why don't you join us?' the woman with the plaits and teeth had said to him.

'Join you?' he'd replied, glassy eyed.

'Here's my card. In case you fancy it.'

Dad must have decided that he did fancy it and phoned the number on the card, and when she told him where she

was, he jumped into his Help the Aged beads and sandals and chugged off to join her. At the wood.

The very wood my mother and Audrey Mint were racing towards on public transport!

I had to act. Not to protect Dad, who deserved everything Mum was bound to lob at him, but for me, because I don't like living in a war zone. I fished in the little black book by the phone for his mobile number. I thumbed the digits. There were a few rings, then this smooth recorded voice told me that Dad wasn't available. I said 'Thanks a lot,' and hung up. He'd either switched his phone off or his battery was flat. My father's fate was sealed. Mine too. Life at *The Dorks* was going to be total misery until the day I put the Golden Oldies in a home.

CHAPTER SIXTEEN

All I could do was wait for my parents to put in an appearance, and hope they didn't put in the same appearance. They didn't. Mum came in first. I knew she'd caught Dad out from the way her face was set in concrete.

'Let's see the "I'm an Old Fart" badge then,' I said cheerily.

'Don't talk to me,' she snapped.

'OK,' I said and mouthed 'What's for tea?'

She threw a concrete scowl my way. 'What?'

I mouthed it again.

'Jiggy,' she said, 'I'm not in the mood, what did you say?'

'You told me not to talk to you,' I said out loud.

'Say it anyway.'

'I said "What's for tea?"'

'Tea?' she said. 'Is that all you can think about at a time like this?'

'A time like what?'

The fists hanging at her sides

138

developed extra knuckles and she took a very deep breath.

'I've sent your father to the Chinese.'

'Really? Have the Chinese asked for him?'

'For a takeaway,' she said with a voice so icy it froze my hair.

'The Chinese want him for a takeaway?'

Later I got the full gist of what had happened, in bits and pieces like I usually do, by paying careful attention to the things they didn't say to one another, which was quite a lot. It had all gone the way I thought it would. Dad had hared off to share a placard with toothy Serena at Ingle Woods, and shortly afterwards Mum and Audrey arrived and caught him. I was glad I wasn't in Dad's shoes, and not only because they're too big for me.

Dad came in about half an hour later, bearing a brown paper bag. 'I suppose you've heard,' he said with a heavy scowl.

'All I've heard is a lot of banging about upstairs. I think Mum's trying to destroy the place. I've put the

chopsticks on the trays.'

'Chopsticks?'

'For the Chinese.'

'Trays?'

'It's Saturday. The weekend. Tea in front of the telly.'

'Oh. Yeah.'

I went to the foot of the stairs. 'Mum!' I yelled up. 'The silage is here!' I was halfway to the kitchen when I realised that she might not have understood this and went back. 'I mean the food, not Dad!' I started away again, then had another thought, and went back again. 'But he's here too!' I finally made it to the kitchen, where Dad was taking a stack of cartons out of the brown paper bag.

'Doesn't smell very Chinesey,' I said.

'It's a curry,' he said.

'I thought you went to the Chinese.'

'I did. It's a Chinese curry.'

'Do the Chinese eat curry?'

'Haven't a clue, but they make it.'

'Does Mum know?'

'That the Chinese make curry? Don't s'pose she cares right now.'

'I mean does she know you've got a

curry?'

'Does it matter? She eats curry.'

'Not usually Chinese.'

'What difference does it make? A curry's a curry.'

'Not necessarily. There are all sorts of curries.'

'All the same to me,' he said.

'But probably not to Mum. My guess is you've just earned yourself an extra stretch in the dog house.'

He sighed. 'Hardly ever out of it these days.'

For the second time in as many hours, I was right about the way things would go. Mum's jaw practically broke her chest bone when I handed her the tin tray with the bowl of curry and Chinese poppadoms on it.

'What's this?'

'A tray,' I informed her.

'This *food*.'

'Yung Foo Vindaloo.'

'Vindaloo?' she said.

'Only guessing. No expert.'

She looked at Dad. With difficulty. Her eyes didn't seem to want to go that way, and when they arrived they didn't seem to want to focus.

'Why didn't you get a proper Chinese?'

His eyes had as much trouble turning and focusing on her. I think only one of them managed it. 'You didn't *say* get a proper Chinese.'

'I would have thought it was *obvious*.'

They dipped their heads and started forcing Yung Foo Vindaloo through the drawbridges guarding their mouths. Didn't look easy. Wasn't easy for me either, because I'd forgotten to switch the chopsticks for forks. My favourite parents sat at opposite ends of the couch, with a person-sized space between them. I sat in the armchair behind the door. I was almost out in the hall but it had to be better than sitting between those two when the knives were out. Or the chopsticks.

Stallone was in the room too, squatting between us and the TV but not looking at it. His tail thumped the carpet and he glared at us with his mean green eyes. You could read his catty mind. 'Where's *my* Yung Foo

142

Vindaloo then?' he was thinking. He does that all the time, stares hungrily at the food on your plate. Puts you off a bit. How would he like it if I hung around his mog bowl eying his Jellied Cat-O-Meat?

The TV sound was turned down, so you couldn't hear a thing, but there was this man being interviewed by this type in a suit, and the man being interviewed had the hairiest nose I ever saw. This hair was so thick and long that it looked like weeds that had been secretly growing behind his eyes since the last time he blew his beak. This set me wondering. What happened when he had a cold? Did all the gunge run into the nose hair? And did the nose hair get all tangled and stiff so he had to pick the stuff off when it was dry? And what if there were sub-zero temperatures when the hair was still wet? Did the hairs separate and stand out like sparklers? These were important questions, and I was pretty sure the interviewer wasn't asking any of them.

I shook myself by the shoulder and

slapped myself round the face. I was becoming obsessed with all things nosy. But then I wondered why I'd never become obsessed with them before. I mean, think about it. Nostrils are everywhere. You can't move for the things. There were eight of them in our living room, if you count Stallone's. I became dimly aware that the owner of one pair (Mum) had just muttered, 'Could hardly keep your hands off her, could you?' to the owner of another pair (Dad), who was going quietly insane trying to pick up a grain of Yung Foo rice with his chopsticks.

'You imagined it,' he muttered back.

'I imagined nothing. How long have you known her?'

'I don't know her.'

'She seemed to know you.'

'I have one of those faces.'

'So does she, the way you were virtually licking it.'

'Oh, eat your Chinese.'

'Chinese!'

'Curry then.'

'Curry!'

'I can't do much right, can I?'

144

'Well you're right about *that*,' said Mum.

'I think it's pretty good,' I said from my chair behind the door.

Three pairs of eyes looked my way. One pair was Stallone's.

'What?'

'What?'

'Meow?'

'The Yung Foo Vindaloo. Cool. In a hottish sort of way.'

'Quiet,' said Mum, turning the TV up with the remote she'd been sitting on so no one else could get at it. 'I want to hear about this bath oil.'

Now all of us except Stallone sat eating Yung Food Vindaloo and watching adverts. Not for long, though.

'This is ridiculous,' Dad growled after we'd learnt all there was to know about the bath oil, cars no one can afford, and insurance for when you die. 'We do *not* need to watch adverts over tea.'

'Better than watching my husband drool over every attractive bit of stuff he sees,' Mum said.

Dad had had enough. He blew his

145

top. Or the Yung Foo Vindaloo blew it, hard to tell.

'Serena, how many more times?! I was being *friendly*, that's all! Isn't friendliness *allowed* anym–?'

He broke off. Silence had fallen with a hearty clunk and all eyes were on at him. Mum's eyes, mine, Stallone's. Even the TV family sharing a really terrific joke about gravy put a cork in it and turned our way for a sec. Dad glanced nervously from one to the other of us, including the gravy family.

'Why are you looking at me like that?'

'You just called me Serena,' Mum said.

'I what? Don't be daft, Peg. You're hearing things now, as well as imagining them.'

'Yes, I'm hearing you call me by your fantasy woman's name.'

Dad put his chopsticks down and moved his tray aside so that it sat on one knee instead of both. Perhaps he felt silly sitting there arguing, with a tray on both knees at once. The word PANIC had appeared in Chinese on his

146

forehead.

'I didn't,' he said, but he didn't sound too sure. 'I didn't.'

'Tell him, Jiggy,' Mum said.

'Leave me out of this,' I said.

Dad looked across at me, pleadingly.

'Put her right, Jig. I said your mum's name, didn't I, nobody else's?'

'Wasn't listening,' I said, and shrugged as if to say, 'Best I can do.'

'Thanks a lot—*Son*.'

Mum got up. 'Here, watch what you want! I've lost my appetite!'

She tossed the remote in my father's lap from a great height. 'Unnnnggh!' he said as his knees jumped and the tray that had been on one of them did an impressive double somersault. As the tray came down with a tinny *doiiing*! on my dad's head, the plate slid off, turned over, and landed on the middle part of the couch.

While Mum stormed out with her tray held high as if she planned to deliver it to a stranger's table, Dad fell to his knees and started dashing Chinese curry off the couch with his sleeve. Somewhere in all this, the

147

remote had changed channels without human help. Captain Picard was glaring at me like this was all my fault.

'This is your fault,' Dad said, agreeing with Jean-Luc as he sleeved Yung Foo Vindaloo on to the floor. Stallone sprang forward to assist, with his tongue.

'My fault?' I said. 'Why, what did I do?'

'You didn't back me up.'

'How could I? We all heard you, clear as day—me, Mum, Stallone, the gravy family. You said Serena.'

He sat back on his heels. 'I did?'

'Clear as a bell. So clear the neighbours must have heard it.'

'God.'

Stallone looked up at him like he almost sympathised with him. In spite of the steam coming out of his ears, he looked happier than usual. Stallone, I mean. Dad didn't look happy. It's not easy to look happy when all the colour in your cheeks has just drained into your shirt.

Suddenly, the phone next to my elbow rang. It does that, that phone.

Rings suddenly, no warning. No considerate build-up starting with a tiny tinkle. No thoughtful whisper like: 'I'm going to ring now, don't wet yourself.' It just rings. Suddenly. And makes you jump. Still, unlike my father I managed not to tip over the remains of my Yung Foo Vindaloo and please the cat.

I grabbed the phone. 'I'm eating!' I yelled at it.

'Jig, it's me.'

Angie. To tell me that Steff had phoned to say that the Snottle had returned.

'Put out the flags,' I said.

'And we're meeting her in the morning at the garden centre. Ten sharp, to try and find out about the seed pod.'

'Ten sharp on a Sunday morning? I don't think so. Ten sharp on a Sunday morning is half way through dreamtime for this McCue.'

'I'll be on your doorstep with Pete at twenty to,' she said. 'If you're not ready and waiting, I'll drag you there in your pyjamas.'

The line died. I wrote a note on my palm to remind me to set my alarm. I know Angie. She has an annoying way of keeping her threats.

*   *   *

Mum went to bed early that night. She does this when she's fed up with one or the other of us. It was only because she wasn't downstairs that Dad summoned the courage to put his new jogging outfit on. I wish he'd warned me, because when I strolled into the hall on my way to the kitchen I thought it was my hero, Captain Neasden, looking out the front door.

'You're going jogging?' I said. 'Now?'

'Thinking about it.'

'Isn't it a bit late?'

'Best time. Dark.'

'Does it have to be dark?'

'I don't want to be seen.'

'Oh, don't be shy, Father. You're not the only jogger in town, I see them all the time, usually in threes.'

'You're right,' he said.

150

'I am?'

'No time like the present.' He took a deep breath. 'Here goes.'

He trotted up the path, looking this way and that in case the neighbours were crouching in force behind their wheelie bins waiting to stand up and video him. The streetlamp by the gate picked him out like a pantomime dame. He opened the gate very quietly and lumbered off into the darkness beyond the sodium, until all you could see of him was the glowing band round his head.

I was in the kitchen a few minutes later stuffing shortbread fingers down my neck, when I heard the front door open. It was Dad, breathing hard.

'You weren't long,' I said.

'Easy stages,' he wheezed, patting his chest. 'Tomorrow the world. Tonight the end of the road.'

CHAPTER SEVENTEEN

'Jiggy, I'm going out!' Mum said, throwing my bedroom door back just as I'm high-stepping into my underpants.

If this has never happened to you, take it from me, the worst thing anyone can do first thing in the morning when you're half in, half out of your pantaloons is appear in your doorway without warning.

'Ho!' I said, as my gusset trapped a toe and I toppled backwards on to the bed, giving my mother an eyeful of the very thing a growing boy doesn't want his mum to get an eyeful of any more.

She was quick, I'll say that for her. Shutting the door on herself, I mean. There was a pause while I heaved the jocks over the ex-privates, followed by a gentle rap at the door. My mother, the rapper.

'Jig, are you decent?' her suddenly tiny little voice said.

'WHAT THE HELL DOES IT MATTER NOW?!' I whispered in

reply.

The door opened nervously. Mum looked in with her hand over her eyes. 'I'm going out,' she said, in case I hadn't heard the first time with all that gusset and elastic work going on.

I grabbed a shirt from the floor. 'What are you telling me for?'

'Well I thought *someone* in this house might be interested in what I do,' she answered.

'You thought wrong. Go! And wipe your mind of everything you've seen so far today!'

She closed the door quietly, like she thought the noise of a door closing at normal volume would upset me even more.

At one minute after nine-forty, I was standing by the front door waiting for Angie to ring the bell.

Brrrrrrrrring!

I lugged the door back.

'You're late!'

'Good morning,' said the two cheery strangers on the step.

'Good morning,' I replied, and shut the door.

'Jig, that was very rude,' Dad said, coming up behind me.

I stood back so he could have a free run at the door. He opened it.

'Good morning,' the two cheery strangers said again. 'May I ask how God figures in your life, sir?' one of them added.

Dad shut the door.

'Father, that was very rude,' I said.

'Didn't know it was that mob,' he said, shuffling into the kitchen.

I hung there waiting for the bell to ring again.

Brrrrrrrring!

I lugged the door back.

'You're late!'

'He wouldn't get up,' Angie said, thumping the nearest shoulder, which I'm glad to say was Pete's. He stood beside her in a big floppy hat that had to belong to his gran.

'You didn't say it was fancy dress,' I said.

'We're going to a *garden* centre,' Pete said, massaging his shoulder with one hand, yanking the hat brim down with the other, and going back up the path

154

with his feet, all at once. Pretty co-ordinated for Pete.

On the way to the garden centre we passed the park. I glanced in. Three joggers were moving steadily along the concrete shore of the boating lake.

'Don't those people have homes to go to?' I said.

'Probably jogging there,' said Angie.

We reached the garden centre and waited at the entrance for the sliding doors to do their stuff. These doors are such slow sliders that you wonder if they're in a sulk about doing nothing but opening and closing for people all the time. You have to see their point. If you were a sliding door wouldn't you get sick of just going *swiiiish-swiiiish* all day, every day? I mean, it might be a really nice day and you're thinking, 'I'd love a game of tennis right now,' or 'If I wasn't doing this stupid job I could be a ballroom dancer, or a plumber, or eating an ice cream on a beach.' Not much of a life, being a sliding door.

'Where'd you say we'd meet her?' Pete asked Ange.

'Garden centre, that's why we came

155

here, how are the memory classes coming along, Pete?'

'I mean where *exactly* at the garden centre?'

'We didn't discuss where exactly.'

'Big place,' I said.

'She'll be here somewhere.'

'Hey, it's that geezer,' said Pete.

'What geezer?'

'The one from the woods.'

The geezer was looking at young trees in the Young Trees section and jotting things in a notebook. We would have scooted by without a word, but he looked up too soon.

'You three,' he said.

'You one,' I said.

'Shopping for trees?' Angie asked.

'Doing some sums.'

And that was it. End of chat.

'See you!' we cried after we'd all got fed up of staring at our feet.

We moved along. No sign of Steff. Plenty of growing things with price tags, but no Steff.

'She could be anywhere,' said Pete.

'Stop whingeing,' said Ange.

'I'm not whingeing, I'm just saying

she could be anywhere.'

'Well don't.'

Suddenly a tall, leafy, potted thing stepped out from some bushes. 'What are you lot doing here?' it demanded.

'I don't talk to strange plants,' I said.

My mother nosed the leaves aside. 'You didn't say you were coming here, Jig.'

'Nor did you.'

'What do you think of my Bird of Paradise?'

'What Bird of Paradise?'

She jiggled the big pot plant in her hands. 'This one.'

'I know the old bloodshots are a bit over the hill,' I said, 'but if you thought you were buying a bird you were done.' I flicked one of the leaves. 'Leaf, not feather. Take a squint.'

'Can't you see why it's called a Bird of Paradise?'

'No.'

'I can,' said Angie.

'You can?' I said.

'Any moron can.'

'Not this moron.'

'Nor this one,' said Pete.

157

'Look at it,' said Angie.

'I thought we were,' I said.

'Look properly.'

Pete and I stood back and looked properly. The leaves were sort of spear-shaped, and growing up out of them was this long green stem. At the top, the long green stem turned bright yellow and leaned over and came to a point, kind of like a beak. On top of the beaky bit this arrangement of red and purple stood up like a plume. On a head.

I nodded. 'Bird of Paradise. Yeah. Cool.'

'Just looks like a plant to me,' said Pete.

'Every moron but one,' said Angie.

Mum went on her way and we went on ours, and in a minute we saw Snonker sitting in the Garden Furniture area on one of those long swinging seat things with a canopy. She stopped swinging when we got to her.

'Nose running,' Pete said.

'Yes,' she said happily. 'He'll be up for a snack in a minute.'

It was a warm day, but her coat was

158

closed over the bump on her chest. She unbuttoned the top bit. An eye looked out at us.

'Hi, ugly,' said Pete.

The Snottle reached for Steff's chin and hauled himself up her face like a little round mountaineer. It licked her top lip. Steff smiled. So did Angie. I didn't smile. Nor did Pete. Pete stuck his fingers down his throat. For once I was with him. I've never understood how people can stand being licked by their pets. Dog lovers are the worst. Even big tough macho types go all soft when their stupid mutt decorates their chops with saliva, usually two seconds after licking his nuts [The dog's nuts.]. I can't look when I see that. I don't even want to *think* about it.

'How did you get him back?' I asked as the Snottle dropped down and perched on the seed pod.

'I went back to that rubbish dump,' Steff said.

'The Midden.'

'The Midden. And he must have seen me, because suddenly there he was, bouncing up and sucking my nose.'

She stroked the Snottle, who gazed up at her making soft wolf-whistley sounds that gradually turned into a kind of high-pitched purr.

'Can we just get this over with and skedaddle?' Pete said from the shadow of his gran's hat brim.

For the second time I was with him, and agreeing with Pete that many times in a row is pretty rare, believe me. Point was, you never knew who was lurking among the rhodadoodahs and chrysanthedads. Bryan Ryan or someone like him might have followed us and be taking pictures of us with flowers and girls that very minute.

'Wish I'd worn a hat,' I said, eyeing Pete's enviously.

He pulled the brim down further still and walked on. 'Learn to think ahead, son, like yours truly.'

He said this just half a step before he crashed into a lamppost.

CHAPTER EIGHTEEN

The girls took the lead, as girls usually do, and Pete and I followed, as we usually do, but at a distance so people wouldn't think we were with them. Not so far behind that we couldn't hear what they were saying, though. Angie asked Steff how yesterday's demo went and Steff said it went OK but it was probably wasted, like all the others, because the developers still planned to start work tomorrow.

'Not much fun for you, standing around out there with no chance of changing anything,' Angie said.

'Well, we had a bit of a laugh yesterday,' Steff said. 'This middle-aged loon in beads drove up and started making eyes at my mum and asking if he could share her placard.'

'Your . . . mum?' I said, from behind.

'Yes,' Steff said, flipping round and walking backwards. 'And his wife turned up shortly afterwards with a friend and got really ratty with him.'

I smiled feebly. 'Must have been a scream.'

'It certainly perked our day up.'

Steff and Angie led the way to a wooden hut with an open door and a sign saying GARDENING & PRODUCT ADVICE. Inside, there were all these shelves with plant books for sale and reference, and posters of TV gardening stars on the walls. There was also a desk with a pile of papers on it, and a mug of cold tea with a dead bluebottle floating on top, and there was a grey filing cabinet, but there was no one to hand out the Gardening & Product Advice.

'We could try looking it up ourselves,' Steff said.

She'd tucked the Snottle back in her coat while walking through the garden centre, but as there was no one in the hut she let him grope his way out again. He sat there looking hopefully up her nose, and humming in this weird little way he had.

Angie took down a reference book. 'What would it be under?'

Steff shrugged. 'Pods?'

162

They were still trying to find 'pods' in the index when someone came in. Female, thirtyish, yellow badge on her chest with the garden centre name in blue.

'Help you?'

'Are you the Gardening & Product Advice expert?' Angie asked while Steff turned away to stuff the Snottle back under cover.

'I do my best.'

'We're trying to find out what sort of plant comes from . . . this.'

She waited till Steff had buttoned up before reaching for the seed pod and holding it up, still around Steff's neck.

The Gardening & Product Advice person noticed the bump under Steff's coat and glanced round to see if we'd nicked anything. When she couldn't find anything missing, she looked at the pod.

'New one on me. Where did it come from?'

'It was my nan's,' Steff said. 'I don't know where she got it.'

Another garden centre person came in. Could have been the woman's

163

double except his hair and skin colour were different, he was shorter, wore glasses, and was male. He even wore a badge like hers.

'Ever seen one of these before, Bernie?' the woman asked.

Steff untied the shoelace round her neck and handed the seed pod to Bernie. Bernie's eyes sort of jumped behind his glasses when he saw it. 'Crikey Moses,' he said, turning the pod over in his hands. Then he sniffed it. His nose immediately started to run. The bump under Steff's coat jumped excitedly. Steff turned away, holding her coat tight at the neck and chest. The female Gardening & Product Advice person frowned at the bump.

'What is that?'

'My kitten.'

'You're not supposed to bring pets here.'

'Oh, I didn't know that. Sorry. But I'll keep him inside my coat.'

Bernie held the pod up to the light as if he expected to see through it. 'I haven't come across one of these in donkey's years.'

164

We all exchanged glances. Then we took them back again.

'You've seen one before?' Angie said to Bernie.

'Saw a lot of 'em at one time. Down Ingle Woods way. We called them splatter eggs.'

'Splatter . . . eggs?'

He looked at us. A thick glob of nose sap hung from each of his nostrils. 'Yes. Me and me mates would go on splatter hunts, and when we found them we'd jump on 'em.'

'It's an *egg*?' said Steff, taking it back from him in wonder.

'You didn't know?'

'No, I thought it was a . . . never mind.'

'It doesn't look like an egg,' Angie said.

'But it is.'

'What did you jump on them for?'

Bernie grinned. 'Well, you know . . . boys.'

Ange glared at me and Pete. 'Oh, we know *boys*.'

'I never jumped on an egg,' I protested.

'Me neither,' said Pete. 'Give it here.'

Steff folded her hands protectively around the pod—egg—like it was suddenly three times as fragile as before.

'Why did you call them splatter eggs?' Angie asked Bernie. 'I mean why *splatter*?'

'Because when you crushed them all this green slime splashed out. Had to jump away quick or it was halfway up your legs. Smelled awful. Like a stink bomb. We took one to school once, and Dylan Ryan stomped on it in class, and—'

'Ryan?' I said.

'—and the stench was revolting in that confined space. Took a week to wear off.'

'Your nose is running,' said Pete.

'Oops!' Bernie whipped out a handkerchief. 'Forgot about that. Your nose always ran when you got near them. Still does, obviously.'

'Why do you think that is?' Steff asked, mopping her own nose.

'I'm guessing it's some sort of

166

protective mechanism,' Bernie said through his hanky. 'A repellent built into the eggs that affects the mucus membranes of predators.'

'Didn't put you lot off,' Angie said.

He tucked his hanky away. 'You do things like that when you're a kid. Wouldn't now.'

'Glad to hear it.'

'Did the eggs break easily when you jumped on them?' I asked him.

'Oh, far from it. You had to come down on them with all your weight, with your heel, and even then it could take two or three goes. That's not your standard eggshell there.'

The female Gardening & Product Advice person had gone behind the desk to flip through a big reference book and pretend she wasn't listening. She looked kind of teed off actually, probably because we were taking up valuable floor space and not talking about plants.

'Were there any left by the time you stopped splatting them?' This was Pete. Quite a sensible question for him, but because it was Pete it was hard to tell if

he cared what had happened to the eggs, or if he wanted to know where others might be so he could splat them himself.

'I'm sure there were,' Bernie said. 'There didn't seem to be a shortage. Splatter a batch one night and the next there'd be others there in their place. But one evening this old biddy was waiting for us and she chased us off with a stick, and next time we went on a splatter hunt there weren't any to be found.'

'Old biddy?' said Steff.

'Lived in the woods. Fierce as a grizzly but a fraction of the size. Terrified of her, we were. Thought she was a witch.'

'You think she hid the eggs from you?'

'She must have. Never saw any again after she chased us off.'

'Ever see what was inside the things?' Pete again.

'Apart from the green slime, no. Never gave it a thought, as I recall. Again, I'd be more curious these days.'

'When you were around them,' Steff

said, 'did you ever . . . sneeze?'

'Sneeze? I should say so. But these weren't ordinary sneezes. They were real *honks*. And when we honked, this stuff would shoot out of our noses, and—'

'Bernie!'

Bernie broke off. His female double, the other Gardening & Product Advice person, was frowning at him from behind the desk.

'You shouldn't fill these kids' heads with this garbage.'

Bernie looked a bit embarrassed. 'Yeah. You're right. I shouldn't.'

Angie leaned towards him. 'Garbage? Is that all this is?'

He hesitated, glanced at his happy workmate, then said, 'Outside.'

We went out, all of us except the woman. When we were a bit away from the hut, Steff asked Bernie if he'd ever seen any moving pictures in the nose stuff. Bernie's eyes turned into billiard balls. The white ones with the little black dots.

'You know about the moving pictures?'

169

'I sneeze sometimes,' Steff said, 'I mean *really* sneeze—'

'Snonk,' I said.

'—and when I sneeze—snonk—I see stuff in it when it lands. We all do.'

'Not all,' said Pete. He sounded quite pleased about this.

'We have things to talk about,' Bernie said. 'Let's find somewhere to sit.'

CHAPTER NINETEEN

Bernie led us past gurgling water features, and piles of multi-coloured paving slabs, and displays of pots marked SPECIALS, to a fenced-in area full of stone lions, stone gnomes, stone hedgehogs, and stone goddess types with their woojahs hanging out. There was even a stone bench, and Bernie said we could sit on it but he couldn't because he was supposed to be working, and sitting down wasn't allowed except at tea break and it wasn't time for one of those. We asked him what sort of pictures he and his mates used to see in the snonk stuff.

'Something bad,' he told us. 'Always something bad. Nothing fatal, but bad enough—falling over a tree root, getting caught in a sudden downpour, chased by the old biddy, things like that. And then it would actually happen, exactly as we saw it. Is that your experience too?'

'Pretty much,' said Steff.

'Any idea what it's all about?' Angie asked him.

'The eggs,' he said. 'Extra protection. That's my guess anyway. If they can make noses run, who's to say they can't give you a glimpse of something that's going to happen to you and make it happen?'

'But why always something bad?' I said.

'To scare us off. Keep us away. The animal world's full of weird and wonderful creatures. The skunk turns its back end on unfamiliar visitors and sprays them with foul-smelling liquid; some species of chameleon change their look and colour to blend in with their surroundings . . .' He trailed off.

'I wonder what kind of creature would come from an egg like this?' Steff said, stroking the ex-seed pod.

'You'll find out soon enough,' Bernie said.

'I will? How?'

'Because that one's close to hatching. Very close.'

'Hatching?'

'Look.'

We crowded round. A thin line had appeared in the egg and green slimy stuff was oozing out. Every nose that wasn't already running, started. There was a lot of sniffing.

'We ought to go and put it somewhere safe,' Steff said. She glared at Bernie. 'Away from *people*.'

'I wouldn't harm them now,' Bernie said. He sounded really sorry for what he and his pals had done.

'Too late for the ones you killed,' Steff said, and got up. She stalked off, one hand round the egg, oozy green slime and all, the other holding her coat closed to keep the Snottle in.

'Thanks,' Angie said to Bernie as we started after her. 'For the advice and all.'

'My pleasure,' he said. 'Will you pop back sometime and tell me what comes out of the egg?'

'Course.'

We never did, though.

When we caught up with Steff she was standing under some hanging baskets examining the egg between her hands. The Snottle was peering at it too, from the slightly open collar of her coat. The line in the egg had widened. Steff's nose was still running but the Snottle seemed more interested in the egg.

'What should we do with it?' Steff asked.

'Put it on the ground,' Pete said.

'Why?'

He did a little clodhopping, stomp-stomp-stomp dance.

'You're an idiot, Garrett,' Angie said to him.

'Jo-king,' he said.

'Yeah, well if that's the best you can come up with, get lost.'

'Say no more,' Pete said. 'I know when I'm not wanted.'

'At last!' Angie cried.

'I only came along to be friendly. You think I want to hang out with a couple of girls in a place that sells flowers? No boy would. Come on, Jig.'

'I want to see what comes out of the egg,' I said.

'Correction,' Pete said. 'Three girls in a place that sells flowers.'

He swaggered away, hands in

pockets, kicking pebbles on the path. We watched our old friends the sliding doors *swiiiish* slowly open and let him out. Then we forgot about him.

'It hardly smells at all,' Steff said, sniffing the cracked egg. 'That man said the eggs smelt really horrible when they broke them.'

Two dollops of nose juice plopped on to her hand. The Snottle left it alone.

'Maybe they only smell when stomped on,' Angie said. 'As a kind of payback for the stompers.'

'I think I'd better take it home and keep it warm,' said Steff.

'Risky,' I said. 'No telling what'll come out. Might be something like . . . I don't know . . . a rat?'

'Aaah,' said Steff, all soppy. 'An ickle rat.'

We trotted towards the exit followed by suspicious looks from more staff in green at Steff's chest, which she'd covered up again. We were almost at our old friends the bored sliding doors when Steff stopped suddenly.

'Duck!' she said.

'You want a pet *duck* now?' I said.

She squatted down behind a dwarf sunflower.

'Don't let him see you!'

Ange and I squatted down behind two more.

'Who?'

'Him.'

There were a lot of 'hims' on the other side of the dwarf s-fs. At least half of them were sleepwalking behind women, pushing trolleys full of plants for them. Even the tweedy geezer from the woods was there.

'Let's go,' she said. 'But keep your heads down.'

When the doors finally *swiiirled* open to let us through and we were on the other side, Angie said: 'Isn't that your dad, Jig?'

There was no mistaking that purple spandex and luminous headband. The Help the Aged tracksuit wearer was loping tragically, like a half-cut puppet. Half his strings cut, I mean.

'Never saw him before in my life,' I said.

On the way to Steff's, the egg split

176

even further. 'There's something inside,' she said, squinting into the crack. 'Something moving.'

We were passing the park at this time, so we did a smart left-turn through the gates and found a bench. There was no one about, so Steff unbuttoned her coat and put the Snottle on her knees to give him some air. She held the egg in her hands. The Snottle licked his lips, but even though our noses were practically drowning our chins as we crowded round he didn't leap at us and tuck in. He just sat there gazing at the egg, making little coo-coo-tikka-tik noises.

Suddenly the crack in the egg opened. Green slime spurted, but only a little way, over Steff's hands, not over everything the way Bernie said it did in his day. Maybe it only spurted badly when the eggs were stomped. The main part of the spurt could have been the creature inside being pulped. And there *was* a creature inside Steff's egg. A live creature. We put our heads together over a round green thing the size of a large marble that was

clutching at the air with the tiniest little hands and trying to open its eyes.

'It's a baby *snottle*!' we all whispered at once.

'Prp-prprprp-kikikikikoo,' said Big Snottle.

He must have known all along that it was a snottle egg. He'd been waiting for it to hatch. That could be why he'd gone to the trouble of finding Steff again after the big flush. To be near the egg. It also explained why he seemed so glad to see the egg the first time, and why he was able to park himself on it. Snottle bot, snottle egg: made for one another.

Now the Snottle bounced along Steff's legs to her lap, bump-bump-bump, tiny little bounces, and started licking the slimy green stuff off the baby snottle. And when it was clean . . .

'Hey,' said Steff softly.

. . . he popped it into a pouch that had opened up just under his mouth.

'Like kangaroos,' I said.

'Yes . . .'

We gaped in awe at the two creatures that looked as much like

178

kangaroos as an electric toothbrush looks like a helicopter, until Steff said, 'I think we ought to go to Ingle Woods. That's where the garden centre man and his pals found the eggs. Could be where this one came from too. Where the egg *and* the Snottle came from. Their home.'

'Not for much longer,' Angie said. 'The wood's for the chop, starting tomorrow. In weeks, houses and drainpipes will be springing up all over the place. Nowhere for snottles to go then.'

Steff set the snottles gently down on the bench and squatted on the grass to wipe the slime off her hands. 'Let's take them anyway,' she said.

CHAPTER TWENTY

Our noses had stopped running about the time the egg opened, and no one had any complaints about that. Steff put the two halves of the egg in her bag, carrying the Snottle in her hand now, but still inside her coat so he couldn't be seen. The baby snottle travelled in the pouch under Big Snottle's mouth. Every now and then on the way to the woods we stopped to make sure they were all right. They looked up at us, both of them. Big Snottle was making these happy little koo-koo-kooey sounds now.

'Sweet,' said Steff.

'Yeah,' said Ange.

I just smiled. [Hey, I'm a boy, what do you want from me?]

We were about a quarter of a mile from Ingle Woods when we heard the howl and screech of electric saws.

'No!' Steff cried. 'They can't!'

We speeded up. When we reached the slope down to the woods we saw

half-a-dozen men in helmets and earmuffs, with three saws between them, four trees already down.

'They're not supposed to start until tomorrow!' Steff said.

'They've moved it forward a day to fool everyone,' I said. 'When all the jolly FARTers turn up tomorrow with their megaphones, it'll be too late.'

'Sneaky,' said Angie.

'We have to do something!' Steff said.

'If this was a story instead of real life,' I said, 'this is where the heroes—us—rush down there and do something really smart to outwit the big bad grown-ups and save the day. And there's a nice neat happy ending with us being cheered and other adults standing round with tears of gratitude in their eyes, and there's group-hugging and stuff, and the nasty builders and chainsaw men shuffle off with their heads hung low, defeated.'

'Shut up, Jig,' said Ange.

We weren't the only onlookers. A man had just got out of a Land Rover on the road to our left. Our friendly

181

geezer again. He saw us and raised a hand. 'It's like having an extra shadow,' I said, waving back.

'Mum. Listen.'

We turned. Steff was on her mobile.

'I'm at the woods. They've started cutting the trees down already. What do we do? Get back to me. Better still, round everyone up and come down.' She clicked off. 'I hate leaving messages. I'm always telling her not to turn her phone off, but she keeps doing it, "To save the ozone layer," she says. "Two little batteries will save the ozone layer?" I say to her. "If everyone thought like that," she says, "we wouldn't have a planet left at all."'

'Mothers,' I said. 'World of their own.'

'Well I'm not just *standing* here,' Steff said. She buttoned her coat tight so the snottles couldn't get out and hurtled down the slope shouting, 'Stop! Stop! Stop!'

A couple of the men looked up as she approached, but the rest carried on. Probably couldn't hear her over the screech of the saws, or through the

earmuffs. The men who looked up turned their saw off. Angie and I were still at the top of the slope and we couldn't hear what was being said, but Steff was waving her arms about and stamping her foot, and the two men just stood there, waiting for her to finish.

'You have to hand it to her,' Angie said.

'Yes,' I said. 'Might as well leave her to it.'

'Leave her to it? You mean . . . desert her?'

'Absolutely. Come on.'

I started to leave.

'Jiggy McCue, get back here at once!'

I got back there at once. Angie started down. So did I.

'We have a job to do,' one of the men was saying to Steff when we got there. 'We can't stop on your say-so.'

'Oh, I see,' she replied, 'so you'll cheerfully destroy a wood that's been here for centuries for a bit of money, is that it?'

'Double time today,' said the other

sawman.

'And we don't get paid for standing around,' the first man said, glancing up at our friend, the geezer, watching from above.

Just before they turned the saw on again, one of the men said, 'You kids can't hang around here, it's not safe. Go on, away with you.'

The saw started up. Steff tried shouting above the howl, but she didn't stand a chance. They weren't listening now anyway.

'Ah well,' I said to nothing that could hear, and started back the way we'd come, expecting the girls to follow.

After a few steps I realised I was still alone and looked back. Steff had clambered over one of the fallen trees and was walking into the woods. One of the men shouted after her, but she didn't stop. Angie glanced at me, then started after her. I sighed, and tagged along too.

When the noise of the saws was some way behind us I shouted for Angie to wait for me. She didn't, so I got a move on. I had a stitch by the

184

time I caught up with her. I asked her to slow down, but she wouldn't do that either, because she's heartless. Steff was still ahead of us, marching through the woods.

'Where's she going?' I asked. 'And why do we have to go too?'

'Let's just stick with her,' Angie said.

It wasn't a big wood as woods go, but still trees kept getting in the way, which made it a longer walk than I wanted with the bad stitch. And then I got this eerie feeling that we were being followed. I glanced back a couple of times and although I thought I almost saw something there was never anything there. Just trees. In the end I told myself that the feeling of being followed was probably something you always get in woods, and concentrated on keeping my stitch from bursting open.

Eventually this little old cottage crumbled into view. '*Ingle Nook*,' Steff said over her shoulder. 'My nan's place.'

She went into the garden, which was very overgrown, and looked about her

with a frown. 'This is a well,' she said when we joined her.

'A well?' I gasped, holding my stitched ribs with both arms.

She tapped her foot on a patch of leaves which echoed.

'Wooden cover to keep the flies out. Nan didn't have running water, but she used the well water for cleaning the windows, floors, step and things. Had big bottles of water delivered for drinking and washing.'

'I hope that cover's strong,' Angie said. 'You'd get quite a shock if you're skipping along singing a merry tune and you suddenly drop into the ground and drown.'

'There used to be a little fence round it to tell people it was there,' Steff said. 'There's *always* been a fence here.'

'Is this it?'

I'd hobbled over to the cottage for a look in. Under one of the windows, which was broken, I found a bundle of fence posts covered with leaves.

Steff came over. 'Someone must have pulled it up and tried to hide it. The things people do.' She left the

186

mangled fence where it was and went to the little old front door. She tried it. It was locked. 'I hoped for one last look round,' she said sadly.

I reached through the broken window and flipped the catch.

'That's breaking and entering,' Angie said as I slung a leg over the sill.

'The breaking's already been done,' I said.

'Still illegal.'

'I won't tell if you won't.'

Until I jumped down on the other side I still had my stitch. Seconds after I hit the floor, it had gone. How come? Because I suddenly had something else to think about. Something nasty. Very nasty.

CHAPTER TWENTY-ONE

The something nasty was what I'd landed in on the other side of the window. I don't really want to describe it, but take it from me it did not smell good. Fortunately there were some bits of paper about, so I was able to get most of it off my shoe before taking a look round. The room was empty. No furniture, no carpets, nothing at all except a faded old print on one wall—a hay wagon—and rubbish on the floor.

'Can you open the door?' Steff said from the window.

I went out to the hall. There was a pile of free local papers and junk mail on an ultra-dusty rectangle where the doormat used to be. The paper on top was this week's. They even deliver free papers to a cottage in the woods? I thought. Even when the cottage is empty? Even when the ex-owner of the cottage is *dead*?

I kicked the papers aside and twisted the latch. It stuck at first, but I

188

managed it after flexing one of the mighty McCue biceps. Steff came in. Angie followed, kind of nervously. Wasn't like Angie to be nervous, but going into houses she isn't meant to be in isn't something she does a lot of. The bump under Steff's coat was moving about. She opened her coat to give the snottles some air.

'Pongs a bit in here,' Angie said, glancing round.

'Been shut up for a while,' said Steff.

I didn't tell them that it was probably me. My shoe, that is.

While they looked in the downstair rooms, I went to the little kitchen at the end of the hall. The ancient calor-gas cooker was still there, but not smack against the wall, as if someone had tried to rip it out then decided it wasn't worth it.

We didn't say much as we went from room to room. It was too sad. Up the rickety stairs, in the two tiny bedrooms under the sloping roof, there were no beds, no wardrobes, no chests of drawers, not even any light bulbs. Downstairs again, Steff went back to

189

the doorway of the room with the window I'd climbed in by.

'We used to have tea in here,' she said. 'Me and Nan. Mum and I lived quite a way away, so we didn't visit very often, but I came by myself sometimes, by train, and Nan would make these neat little teas for us. Little triangular sandwiches with the crusts cut off. Cheese and cucumber, with mustard-and-cress usually. And jelly for afters. She loved jelly because she could eat it with her teeth out. And jam. Blackberry and raspberry. Smashing. She made it herself. The bread too.'

There was a sound behind us. Someone had followed us in. Someone doing a bad impression of a sentimental violin.

'I thought you'd gone home,' I said.

Pete twirled the rim of his stupid hat. 'Changed my mind. Started for town instead, thought I might bump into someone, but then I saw you three heading for the woods . . .' He looked about him. 'What a dump. Bet your nan was glad to get shot of it,' he said to Steff.

'She didn't get shot of it,' Steff said. 'She died.'

'Same result.'

'She must have been pretty ill,' I said.

'Why?'

'Well . . . to die.'

'She was just old. Ninety-two.'

'Ninety-two! I've got a nan—we call her Gran, though, not Nan—but she's only sixty-something. How come yours was so old?'

'She was really my great nan. I called her Nan because my actual nan, her daughter, died before I was born. Trampled by an elephant at the circus.'

'Trampled by an elephant?' I said. 'You're pulling my trunk.'

'No. She was an elephant trainer.'

'Not a great one by the sound of it,' Pete said. He kicked a small door along the hall. 'What's in here?'

'That's the cellar,' Steff said.

'The cellar? A real live cellar? I've never been in a cellar.'

'I don't think there's anything there. Nan said she used to keep the coal there, but the stairs are very steep and

191

years and years ago the coalman fell down them and refused to carry the sacks down after that, so she put a bunker out back and had it delivered there instead.'

'Bet it's spooky,' Pete said, tugging at the big, rusty bolt. He pulled the door back and looked in. 'Can't see a thing.'

As we joined him at the door, the Snottle became agitated again. Steff undid a couple more buttons of her coat and he squeezed up for a grandstand view just below her chin. Then there was a mini scuffle, and the baby in the snottle pouch jumped up and also peered into the blackness.

Angie laughed. 'Nosy pair, aren't they?'

'Where did the little titch come from?' Pete said in amazement.

'Steff's seed pod,' I told him. 'It was an egg.'

'No!'

'Yes.'

You couldn't see any further than the top four or five steps of the cellar. The rest was in darkness. Weird sort of darkness. Greenish. But suddenly, both

192

snottles burst out of Steff's coat and bounced down the stairs—into the green darkness.

'Oh, now we'll have to go down and *find* them!' Steff said.

'Your fault,' said Angie to Pete.

'That's right, blame me.'

'I already did. Is there a light?' she asked Steff.

'Don't know. Never been down here.' Steff groped for a switch. Found one just inside the door. She flicked it a few times. Nothing.

'Anyone got a match?' Angie said.

No one had. But I'd noticed a box of matches in the kitchen, on the tatty old draining board. I went back for it. It was a big box, for long matches. There were about a dozen unused ones. The rest were dead. I returned to the cellar door. Offered Angie the box. She didn't take it.

'Light one,' she commanded.

I lit a match and we crowded round the doorway. Still couldn't see very far.

'Go down,' Angie said.

'You go down,' I said.

'You're the one with the matches.'

193

I blew the match out, opened her hand, and put the box into it. 'No I'm not.'

She snarled, but lit a match of her own and started down, holding it out before her. 'Your nan was right about these stairs,' she said. 'Steep. Very. No wonder the coalman fell down.'

'Hold the rail,' Steff said, going after her.

'Bit wobbly,' said Angie.

'Better than nothing.'

Pete and I waited at the top while they went down.

'What's it like down there?' I called when they didn't say anything for a while.

'Tuscany,' Angie's voice snapped in the darkness.

'See anything? Anything at all?'

The flame went out. 'No.'

'Try another match,' Pete said.

'Oh, why didn't I think of that?' Angie said sarcastically.

'Lot of sniffing going on down there,' I said.

'My nose is running,' said Ange.

'So's mine,' said Steff.

194

Another match flared.

'Now what do you see?' I asked.

'There's nothing *to* see,' Angie said. 'Can't even see the snottles.'

'Leave them,' said Pete. 'Place gives me the creeps.'

'I thought you were keen to go down there,' I said.

'Past tense.'

There was more silence for a bit, except for heavy girly sniffing down below, then that match went out too. Someone should invent the battery-driven match. Angie lit a fresh one. 'What's that?' she said then.

'Where?' said Steff.

'The floor.'

The match light moved downward. Then Angie said, 'Heeeey,' very softly, and Steff said, 'I don't believe it.'

'Are they what I think they are?' Angie said.

'Have to be,' said Steff. 'And look, some of them are . . .'

'Wow,' said Ange.

'What is it?' I asked. 'What's there?'

'Come and see,' Steff said.

'Can't you just tell me?'

195

'We could, but we're not going to,' Angie said.

The match died. She felt for a new one and struck it. It didn't light. She rummaged for another. This one worked.

'Look at them, look at them!' Steff whispered in an awed voice.

'I'm going down,' Pete said.

'You are?' I said.

'They've found something. Might be gold.'

'You're living in a fantasy world, Pete.'

'Best place to be.' He started down. 'Come on.'

'Someone ought to stay here,' I said.

'Why?'

'Because this is the scene where the four heroic types descend into the haunted blackness and an unseen person slams the door and bolts it.'

'Cluck,' Pete said from halfway down. 'Cluck-cluck-cluck-cluuuck.'

I had no choice. I went after him, slowly, holding the shaky hand-rail. I was about halfway down when the latest match fizzled out. My signal to

196

miss my footing. Miss my footing, slip the last few steps, tip over at the bottom, and land on my hands and knees on the cellar floor (which felt kind of spongy). This, I noticed up close, was where the green glow came from. The floor.

'Angie, another match, quick,' Steff said. 'This is amazing.'

'You've never seen matches before?' Pete said in the dark.

'I think they're all dead,' Angie said.

'No they're not,' Steff said. 'I saw some of them move.'

'I mean the matches.'

As I got to my feet my nose started to run. 'What's going on?' I asked, feeling around in the dark. My fist closed on something.

'I don't know,' said Pete, 'but whoever just gripped my goolies had better let go pretty damn toot-sweet.'

Angie found another match that worked. When she lit it, Pete and I saw what she and Steff had seen. In the thick, soft, greeny stuff that covered the floor, there were dozens of eggs, just like the one in Steff's pocket.

197

Snottle eggs.
Which were hatching.

198

CHAPTER TWENTY-TWO

The eggs that were nearly open were dribbling the same green slime as Steff's egg before the baby snottle popped out. Some of the others were only cracked so far, with the stuff just starting to ooze out. A few hadn't cracked at all yet, but as Angie struck the last matches, a line appeared in each of them, one after the other.

Sniff, sniff, sniff, sniff, sniff, sniff, sniff, sniff, sniff, sniff.

This was us. All four of us. No need to wonder why our brains were suddenly pouring out of our noses. A whole cellar full of snottle eggs!

'You really didn't know they were here?' Angie said to Steff.

'No. But I bet my nan did. I think she put them here to save them from Bernie and his pals. She was the old biddy who chased them. Had to be. How long ago do you think that was? Twenty years?'

'Something like.'

199

'Well I'm guessing that some time after the coalman said he wouldn't risk the steps any more, she gathered up the eggs and put them down here to protect them.'

'They'd have hatched if they'd been down here all that time,' Pete said.

'This is an unknown species,' I said. 'Who knows how long it takes them to hatch?'

'Yeah, but twenty *years*?'

'Unhatched fleas can lie dormant forever,' Steff said.

'We're not talking fleas here,' Pete said.

'No, but . . .'

'But even if it was twenty years,' said Angie, 'isn't it a bit of a coincidence that they hatch the moment we come lumbering down the stairs?'

'Fleas can hatch if someone walks across a floor,' Steff said. 'The vibration.'

'We're not talking *fleas* here.' Pete again.

'Or if the temperature in a room changes,' Steff said.

Pete slapped his forehead.

'Maybe snottles need air and light to hatch out,' I said. 'We open the door, air and light flood in, and . . . crack!'

'My nan must have opened the door a *few* times in twenty years,' Steff said. 'If only to make sure they were all right.'

'She might not have.'

'She would. She was that sort of person.'

The itsy baby snottles had started to roll out of the shells. When they were out they sat there making these cute little clickety-coo noises trying to open their eyes.

'Hey, there's our friend,' I said as Big Snottle dropped from a cobwebby beam. The baby snottle was still in his pouch, little fingers holding on to the edge, eyes peering over. Big Snottle ignored the fact that our noses were running like taps and bounced around the cellar floor licking the slime off the littlies instead.

'Oh, *I* get it,' I said.

'Get what?' said Angie.

'That's why he was so fond of runny nose juice. Reminded him of the stuff

201

that came from . . . snottle eggs.'

'. . . snottle eggs' was said in the dark, because the last match had just gone out.

We didn't leave right away, though. When the faint glow from the floor and the light from the half-open door at the top of the stairs had helped us get used to the dimness, we were able to make out the Snottle going from baby to baby, licking the slime off. At one point the little one in his pouch jumped out and started to do the same, but it kept slipping over and rolling away. This made everyone laugh except Pete, who obviously didn't mean to become a big snottle fan in the near future.

'You know,' he said, 'there could be a reason why the floor's glowing.'

'Oh yeah?' I said.

'Yeah. Radioactive.'

I laughed. 'Radioactive material in an old lady's cottage in the woods? More chance of it being green Kryptonite.'

'If it *is* radioactive,' he said, 'we're in trouble.'

'Snottle dung,' said Angie.

202

'What?' I said.

'I reckon that's what it is. Doesn't it seem likely that where there are snottle eggs there've been snottle adults at one time or other?'

'I thought we'd decided they've been down here since Bernie was a boy,' Steff said.

'Maybe they have,' Angie said. 'But twenty years to hatch? I don't know.'

'Maybe your nan ran a secret snottle farm,' Pete said.

Angie sighed. 'Did you really have to follow us here?'

Pete scowled in the dim light. 'How is it that whenever I say something everyone thinks it's rubbish?'

'Experience,' Angie said.

'How do you mean, snottle farm?' Steff asked him. She wasn't as used to Pete as we were.

'Perhaps the old girl was breeding them,' he said. 'This might just be the latest batch.'

She liked this idea. 'If Nan was keeping them, there could have been oodles of snottle eggs over the years. Generation after generation, all hatching out, growing up, creating dung.'

'If they had something to eat,' I said.

'Maybe snottles only need that slimy stuff. Maybe they make more when they need it and lick it off themselves—or one another.'

'Our snottle seemed happy enough so long as there was plenty of nose stuff to lap up,' Angie said. 'Could be that runny human mucus tastes a lot like snottle slime.'

'Anyone for a taste test?' Pete said.

'And maybe snottle dung is good bedding for the eggs,' said Steff.

'For the adults too,' Angie said. 'We don't know how our little fella got into the Midden—could have got lost ages ago, or dived in there to escape kids who were chasing it, and stayed because some of the muck in it wasn't that different from snottle dung.'

'He didn't seem to mind the voyage round the U-bend,' I reminded everyone, 'and things don't get much more dungish than that.'

'Hey Jig,' Pete said suddenly. 'Your knees. Your hands.'

204

'What's the matter with them?'

'You tell me.'

I held my hands out in front of me. My palms were green. Glowing. I looked down. Knees too, right where I'd fallen when I tumbled down the stairs. And if what I fell into was . . .

'Eeeerrrrhhh!'

I wiped my hands on my jeans like a madman, rubbing and rubbing and rubbing. Even when most of the greeny glow was gone I couldn't bear to close my hands. Pete giggled in the semi-dark. But then it was my turn.

'Pete. Your jeans.'

'What about them?'

'They're glowing too. Right in the hot spot.'

He looked down. 'Oh no! Not there!' He whipped his stupid hat off and started scrubbing at his glowing fly. 'This is your fault McCue.'

'Yep,' I said, cheered up by this happy thought.

More and more of the little snottles were rolling out of the eggs now. Once they were licked clean by Big Snottle they just sat there chuckling quietly and looking about them, as if wondering what kind of world this was and what you did for laughs on your days off.

'I don't get it,' Steff said. 'There was nothing in Nan's will about eggs or creatures in the cellar. What did she think we would do when we found them?'

'Maybe she left instructions somewhere,' I said.

'If she did we missed them, but we only came here once after the funeral, to take a few mementoes away, photo albums and stuff. Then Mum asked some house clearance people to cart the rest awa—'

'Quiet!' Angie hissed.

We fell silent. Funnily enough, so did the snottles. Footsteps overhead. There was someone upstairs.

'Hello! Anyone down there?'

There were a few dozen snottles down there, and four humans in the prime of kidhood, but you'd never know it from the shortage of Yesses to that question.

The door at the top of the stairs

206

closed. We heard the bolt being drawn. 'Never fails,' I said.

Even with the door closed it still wasn't completely dark. As well as the faint glow from the floor there were now all these tiny little points of light. Baby snottle eyes. But this wasn't the time to admire the eyes of exotic species that live in dung. Our only exit was cut off. We were trapped. The next bit of daylight we saw, and the next fresh air we breathed, would be when the demolishers moved in and we became part of the rubble.

'I'm not staying here,' Pete said in the greeny murk. We vaguely saw him moving across the room.

'Mind the snottles!' Steff cried in alarm.

'It's them who'd better mind me,' he barked.

'Ooh,' said Angie.

'Ooh what?' said Steff.

'I think I'm going to sneeze.'

'Me too,' I said.

'And me,' said Steff.

'Hold on to your wigs!' bawled Pete, not wanting to be outdone.

We threw our heads back and snonked. All four of us, simultaneously. Four-snonk harmony.

CHAPTER TWENTY-THREE

Oh boy, what a snonk. The Crown Prince of Snonks. In that underground cellar our four-in-one snonk was ten times louder than it would have been out in the open. Must have terrified the baby snottles because the light from all their little eyes went out in a single wink.

But it wasn't just the noise. I mean not *only* noise. Oceans of nose juice spurted from eight nostrils on to the walls—all four walls, because without talking it over we'd all turned in different directions and snonked on different walls. Then, glowing faintly, just like the snottle slime, the stuff crept to the corners and joined up with the gunk on the other walls. And a picture appeared. A single picture, all around us.

'It's true!' gasped Pete. 'You can see things in it!'

'Glad you finally caught up,' I said.

The picture wasn't terrifically clear,

209

because it was so gloomy down there, but we could just make out trees, lots of trees, and the cottage we were in, and . . .

'Us!' said Angie.

Us, standing together outside *Ingle Nook*'s front door. But then the picture went sort of hazy, and it was hard to tell if anyone was still by the door, and something was happening in the garden. Someone who could have been any one of us was falling into the old well that no longer had a warning fence round it to tell people it was there.

'Who went down the well?' Angie said.

'Looked like Pete to me,' I said.

'What well?' said Pete.

'Definitely Pete,' I said.

'I thought it was me,' said Steff.

'What well?' said Pete.

'Looked more like Jig to me,' said Ange.

'There's a well in the garden?' said Pete.

'Yes, there's a well in the garden,' said Steff.

'It can't have been me,' I said. 'I

know where it is, and if we ever get out of here I'm not going near it.'

'Could be dark by the time we get out,' said Pete. 'If it's dark you might not see the well and go down it anyway.'

'If we're still locked in this cellar by the time it gets dark,' I said, 'our parents will have called Crimewatch, and reconstructions of our last movements will be on everybody's telly.'

'I hope I'm played by someone handsome,' said Pete.

'No chance,' I said. 'These things have to be true to life.'

The icky liquid on the walls was dribbling slowly down to the floor, taking the cellarama picture with it. Suddenly, baby snottles were bouncing to all four walls and lapping up their first big meal. We might have been fascinated to watch them if we hadn't been locked in.

'We have to get out of here,' Pete said.

He started up the stairs and would have hammered on the door with his

211

fists, but before he got to the top we heard the bolt being pulled back. Pete froze as the door opened.

'Who's down there? I know you're there, I heard you.'

'There's four of us,' Angie said. 'We're coming up.'

'What are you doing down there?' the man in the doorway asked as we trooped up. 'Why didn't you answer the first time?'

'Didn't know you were going to lock us in,' Pete said, reaching the top.

Angie was just behind him, but three-quarters of the way up, she stopped and whispered down to Steff and me. 'What about the snottles?'

'What about them?' Steff said.

'They'll be killed when the cottage is knocked down.'

'Maybe not,' I said.

I was last on the stairs and before starting up, I'd taken a final look round. The cellar was empty. No snottles, big or small. All that was left to show they'd been there were the empty egg cases and the slightly glowing floor.

'Where have they gone?' Steff whispered.

'Into the dung,' I said. 'Into the floor probably.'

'Through concrete?' said Angie.

'Might not be concrete. It's an old building.'

'I didn't say goodbye to my friend,' Steff said. 'I'll never see her again, and I didn't say goodbye.'

'Her?' I said.

'Of course. Did you ever see a male make so much fuss of babies?'

'Hello,' Angie said to the man, when we got to the top. 'What are you doing here?'

It was our pal, the tweedy geezer. Again.

'I saw you go into the woods. Thought I ought to warn you that it's not safe, with all the trees coming down and the work that's planned. How did you get in here? The door should be locked.'

'Broken window,' I told him. 'Our friend here wanted a last look at her nan's old place before it's pulled down.'

'Your nan's?' he said to Steff.

213

She turned away from him. She looked pretty sour. 'Don't you know who this is?' she said to us.

'Some man we met in the woods,' said Pete.

'Some man you met in the woods,' Steff repeated.

It was the way she said it. Suddenly 'some man we met in the woods' didn't sound too cute. If my mother had been there she would have shrieked, thrown her arms in the air, and called the police.

'He's the one who bought the wood from whoever owned it,' Steff said. 'And the cottage from Mum after Nan died. He's the one who's destroying the trees and building a horrible new housing estate.'

'You?' Angie and I said in amazement. Pete just nodded, like he'd suspected this all along, which he hadn't.

'The houses won't be *that* bad, I hope,' the geezer said.

'Designed by postmen,' said Pete.

The man looked puzzled. 'Postmen?'

'Or picture framers, flower

arrangers, motor mechanics.'

'Sorry, I don't . . .'

'And we thought you were one of the good guys,' Angie said.

He smiled. 'I'm just a businessman trying to make a living.'

'By destroying natural habitats and ancient forests,' said Steff.

'I'll be planting more trees on the new estate. And there'll be grassy areas for the kids to play on.'

'Not *quite* the same,' Steff muttered.

The geezer led the way out into the garden. The light was blinding after the cellar. He took a key from his pocket and locked the front door.

'Better not hang around here,' he said. 'I can't guarantee your safety if you do. Take care now.'

He walked away through the overgrown garden. I glanced at Angie. She looked as disappointed as I felt. I could read her mind. How nice he'd seemed before we knew who he wa—

A sharp splintering sound, followed by a sharp yelp, and the geezer plunged feet first into the ground.

'It wasn't one of us, after all,' said

215

Steff.

It was a very narrow well, and not a very deep one, just wide and deep enough for one man to stand in with his arms straight up over his head. This was handy for the geezer, because that's exactly what he was doing.

'You all right?' Angie asked, leaning over the well.

'No, of course I'm not bloody all right,' he said angrily. 'There should be a warning fence there. Was last time I looked. Help me out.'

'Say the magic word,' said Pete.

'Prosecution!' growled the geezer.

'That's the one,' Pete said.

'In a story,' I said, as we reached for our ex-friend's raised hands and arms, 'this is where the big bad developer is so grateful to the young heroes for rescuing him that he changes his mind about destroying the wood and knocking down the old cottage, and there's an ending so soppy you want to throw up all over the duvet.'

'Will you stop that?' said Angie, glaring at me.

The geezer wasn't grateful. Not one

bit. He thought it was us who'd trashed the fence. Last we saw of him he was stomping off, soaked from hips to socks, muttering nasty things about us. No mention of a reward for hauling him out, no promises not to build the houses or blitz the wood. Not even a group hug.

CHAPTER TWENTY-FOUR

The phone rang around midday. That is, every non-mobile in the house rang around midday, like they'd got together and planned it over a beer. I was just passing one of them on my way to the kitchen.

'Answer it, will you, Jiggy,' my mother said from the upstairs landing.

'There's a phone three steps to your left,' I reminded her. 'It's that thing on the wall that looks like a dead fish.'

'You are so *unhelpful* sometimes!' she said, dropping the bundle of washing she'd been about to bring down. She seized the wall phone. I hung around at the foot of the stairs in case it was for me. 'You're *where*?' I heard her say. 'What are you doing at the police station? What have you *done*?'

'Woh!' I said, and grabbed the hall phone.

'I haven't done anything,' Dad's little voice said at the other end of the line.

'It's what's been done *to* me.'

'So what's been done *to* you?'

'I've been mugged.'

'Mugged?'

'I was jogging in the park. They came at me out of the blue. Three of them.'

'Hang on,' Mum said. 'You were . . . jogging?'

'Yes.'

'You?'

'I bought a tracksuit specially.'

'You bought a tracksuit? *You* bought a *tracksuit*?'

'Couldn't find the nerve to show her, eh, Dad?' I said.

'Jiggy, get off the line,' Mum snapped, glaring down the stairs at me.

'OK.' But I didn't.

'Let me get this straight,' my mother said, not to me. 'You bought a tracksuit, you went jogging, and you were mugged?'

'Yes.'

'Did you see their faces?'

'I wasn't looking at faces. It took all my concentration to stop my heart exploding. What berk invented jogging

anyway? Hope they threw him off a cliff.'

'Did they get anything?' Mum asked.

'Who?'

'Your muggers.'

'*My* muggers? They weren't *my* muggers. You make it sound like I adopted them.'

'Did they take anything *from* you?' Mum said.

'Yes. My headband.'

'You have a headband as well as a tracksuit?'

'Had. Don't now. The sods.'

'But that's all they took, your headband?'

'It was all I had.'

'You were lucky then,' Mum said.

'Lucky?' said Dad. '*Lucky*?! I haven't won a raffle, Peg. I've been mugged! By joggers!'

CHAPTER TWENTY-FIVE

The Fellowship of Ancient Rights for Trees had lost the battle for Ingle Woods, but they soon found some other trees to get worked up about. Angie went round Steff's a couple of times, but with the Snottle gone they didn't really have much in common. That was OK though, because once Steff stopped sniffing and snonking she soon found new friends. The only other time the four of us were together was one evening a few weeks after the Big Snonk in the cellar. I'd gone over to P & A's to see if their lives had become more interesting since I last checked, and Steff was there. She was wearing something round her neck that I never expected to see again. The snottle egg.

'I put a little picture of Nan inside before I glued it back together,' she said. 'I can't see her, but I know she's in there. It's like having her with me wherever I go.'

Pete and I exchanged manly smirks.

Girls. So sentimental.

Angie suggested that as we were all together again we ought to go see how they were getting on with the executive houses. Steff wasn't keen. Didn't care how they were getting on, she said. But we went anyway, for something to do. Pete took his bike, and kept spinning on ahead, then coming back and riding round us with his hands behind his head, going 'Wahoo! Wahoo!' for some reason. To take my mind off the fact that one of my best friends was a total moron, I asked Steff if she missed the Snottle.

'Well,' she said, 'I moped around the house for a couple of days after she went, and when Mum asked what was up I said something pitiful like, "I wish I wasn't so alone all the time," and when one of the nicer strays from the street wandered in, not much more than a kitten really, she said I could keep him, but only if he wanted to stay.'

'And did he?' Angie said.

Steff showed her teeth. They were very bright, just like her mother's.

Funny I never noticed that before.

'Yes. He follows me round the house. Follows me to school if I let him. So affectionate. And you know what? The way he looks at me. So like the Snottle used to. Gives me quite a turn sometimes.'

'What do you call him?' I asked.

'Snottle.'

We came to the point where the land drops to where the woods used to be. Work had stopped for the day and the builders had gone home. It all looked so different down there now. They'd left a few of the trees at the far end, but the rest had been cut down and cleared away.

'It's gone,' said Steff.

She meant her nan's cottage. It wasn't just gone, it was like it never existed. A number of foundations had been laid, and six of the architect-designed executive houses were already half built. There'd been a story in the local rag about a mysterious allergy the builders had developed. Their noses wouldn't stop running and they kept snonking (the paper called it sneezing,

223

but we knew better). That meant there were still snottle eggs about down there—somewhere.

'Let's see if we can find them,' Steff said.

'I thought you weren't keen on being here,' I said.

'Changed my mind.'

We slithered down the slope. Not easy for Pete with his bike, but at the bottom he climbed into the saddle and shot away while Steff, Angie and I wandered between the foundations and half built houses. No sign of snottle eggs, but when our noses started running we knew they weren't far away. Where, that was the question.

'Hard to tell where your nan's cottage was now too,' Angie said.

'Yes . . .'

Pete rode in and out of standing door frames, singing loudly as we tried to work out where *Ingle Nook* had been. In a minute Steff called out.

'Over here! The ground's softer here. They would have had to fill the cellar in, so maybe the earth's still settling.'

224

'Hope they filled the well in too,' I said, watching where I walked.

When we reached Steff, we saw that her nose was streaming even more than before. Then Angie's and mine were too.

'You know what this means, don't you?' Ange said, sniffing hard. 'Means the snottles came back after the cellar was filled in. Must have felt like it was their personal territory or something. They're down there somewhere, have to be.'

'Watch this!' Pete yelled from somewhere behind us.

He'd hauled his bike up this long plank that was leaning against a ground-floor windowsill, and was sitting in the saddle ready to shoot down.

'You'll do yourself an injury!' Angie shouted.

'Could be an improvement if he lands on his head,' I said. Pete doesn't believe in crash hats.

He zoomed down the plank, legs out like chicken wings. When he ran out of plank, he bumped across the rubble on

225

the slab of concrete that was going to be an executive floor, and hurtled towards us. Stepping aside to let him through, we couldn't miss the ribbons of green goo stretching from his nostrils to his ears via his cheeks. When his front wheel hit a brick, his back wheel bucked and he left the saddle, paddled about in the empty air for a while, and came down in a bed of . . .

Snottles.

Maybe they only came out in the evening, I don't know. There'd been nothing in the paper about the builders seeing little green creatures. All the snottles were smaller than our original one, but about twice the size of the ones we'd watched hatching out a few weeks earlier. Pete didn't realise what he was lying on until some of the snottles threw themselves at his face. Then he let out a shriek. It wasn't a long shriek, mainly because they were smothering him.

'We ought to help him,' I said.

'Give us one good reason,' said Ange.

'Er . . . one for all and all for lunch?'

She glared at me. 'Must you always bring that up?' But sighed. 'Yeah, s'pose so.'

The Musketeers went in. We took our streaming noses to where Pete lay squirming under hungry young snottles, squatted down beside him— on ground that seemed to have developed a slight green glow.

'Come and get it!' Angie said.

Some of the snottles left Pete and bounced on to our faces, and over we went on to our backs. Steff saw the sacrifice we were making for the sake of friendship and must have been impressed, because she also squatted down and invited the snottles to supper. They didn't need a second invitation. Five or six of them immediately landed on her face and tucked in. And there we lay, the four of us, heads covered with little green creatures enjoying a good nosh. The only one who didn't seem to know that we were all getting a facial at the same time was Pete, who kept wailing, 'Why me, why me? Why is it always *me*?'

'It isn't always you, Pete,' I said,

227

spitting out baby snottle tongue. 'It's the lick of the draw.' But he kept on saying it, over and over.

When everything in our skulls had been hauled out through our noses and lapped up, the snottles fell away and sank into the soft earth. In seconds we were alone again. We got up in a hurry before our noses started running again. Pete looked kind of dazed. He grabbed his bike and led the way up the slope. At the top, he swung his leg over the saddle and pedalled off home at full speed. Angie, Steff and I turned for one last look at the building site and what was left of the old woods. The light was fading, which meant that my mother's hair was already turning white with worry. Suddenly Angie said:

'Look!'

We looked. And saw . . .

'The Snottle,' Steff said softly.

A small green object was bouncing from room to room, foundation to foundation, bouncing low, bouncing high, bouncing off walls and cement mixers and anything else it could find. When the Snottle finished showing off,

she bounced on to the roof of a Portaloo where she sat looking at us and—we could just make it out in the silence of the evening—humming quietly.

'For us,' said Steff. 'A snottlish farewell.'

Afterwards, Pete never wanted to talk about that night, and even Angie wasn't keen. But every now and then one of us would give a sharp shudder, or pull a disgusted face, and the others would know why. It did have its funny side though, I have to admit. I mean how many people do you know who get their noses sucked dry by small round creatures that live in glowing green dung?

Well, you know one. McCue's the name . . .

Jiggy McCue

229